Ophelia and T

Deborah Levy was born in Dartington College of Arts, and now lives in London. Her plays include *Pax*, which *City Limits* considered 'remarkable for its combination of intellectual rigour, poetic fantasy and visual imagination', and most recently *Heresies* for the Royal Shakespeare Company, 'an ambitious, imaginative, sometimes funny, sometimes touching, passage across a terrain where moral parables and folk fancies meet' (Marina Warner, *The Independent*). She recently published her first book of poetry, *An Amorous Discourse In The Suburbs of Hell*.

Her first novel, *Beautiful Mutants*, is also published by Vintage.

'Writing of this kind is very risky and the success of Deborah Levy's collection is a tribute to the tight control she keeps on her surrealism and the fastidiousness with which she selects her words. It is no surprise that she is a published poet, because these short pieces have that quality of poetry whereby individual images and ideas often stay with the reader longer than the overall structure'

Punch

'This is [Deborah Levy's] first collection of short stories. With a beautiful rhythm, they make extraordinary reading. Science and love emerge as the conflicting motivations in her complex characters' lives – in the past, present and future'

Guardian

Deborah Levy

OPHELIA AND THE GREAT IDEA

VINTAGE

VINTAGE
20 Vauxhall Bridge Road, London SW1V 2SA

London Melbourne Sydney Auckland
Johannesburg
and agencies throughout the world

First published by Jonathan Cape Ltd, 1988
Vintage edition 1991

'The Sinful Twins' was originally published in *Women's Review*. 'Proletarian Zen' has appeared in *Ambit* and *PEN New Fiction*, 'Heresies' in the *London Magazine* and 'Passion' in *Ambit*. 'A Little Treatise on Sex and Politics in the 1980s' has also appeared in the *London Magazine* and in the *Best Short Stories*, 1987, published by William Heinemann

Phototypeset by Input Typesetting Ltd, London

Printed and bound in Great Britain by
Cox & Wyman Ltd, Reading
ISBN 0 09974820 7

Contents

PREPARING FOR LIFE

AS MAMITA LIES on her back waiting to die (she has predicted the hour of her death long ago), her two daughters, Magda and Terese, are listening to the little handbells Mamita has threaded through her fingers. They are waiting for their sister Rosita, and fear the little bells will stop ringing before she arrives. The air smells of candle wax and muslin.

Terese, the youngest, lies prostrate at the bottom of the stairs leading to Mamita's room. She is dressed in white and weeps. Flies settle on her cheeks. Magda smokes a cheroot and fans herself lethargically.

'Are you weeping yet Magda?' Mamita shouts too loudly for a woman who is dying and for the parched heat of late afternoon.

'Nothing yet Mamita.'

Terese cries extra loudly to compensate for her older sister's apparent lack of feeling. It could be that she just wants to cry.

But Mamita is insistent.

'Try.'

Magda sighs and sticks her sharpest fingernail into her cheek to elicit tears.

'Terese.'

'Mamita?'

'I am anxious that my soul will go roving before I die. Into Manuel's bar for a tapas.'

Magda snorts and shrugs her shoulders. Even that is too much effort in the heat. Terese wipes her eyes.

'But you have closed all the tavernas today Mamita. And you have forbidden the fishermen to go out to sea. So there are no sardines for your soul to feed on.'

Mamita is not satisfied. She knows that when a soul is thirsty it will go a-roving. She wants to have complete control over this, the hour of her death. And she refuses to die before Rosita arrives. Even if it kills me, she says to herself, I will wait.

'Terese. Come and talk with me.'

Terese reluctantly climbs the stairs. Mamita is surrounded by flowers and fruit from neighbours. Her silver hair is coiled immaculately on top of her head. Her nails are buffed and shine like ten half-moons. She has already eaten her way through four golden melons. Terese's eyes are pleasingly red and swollen. Mamita kisses her forehead.

'Last night I heard the cockerels searching for dawn. They couldn't find it.'

'But it came all the same Mamita.' Terese strokes her mother's wrists.

'Yes it came all the same. Leave me now.'

Terese descends the stairs. She cups her hands over her belly and stops half way.

'You mourn for me in white Terese?'

'The colour of ash and bone Mamita.'

She clutches the banister and makes her descent.

'The colour of virgins my angel.'

Magda looks at her sister's belly and stubs out her cheroot.

2

'What if Rosita doesn't come?' Terese sits on the bottom stair.

'Then she doesn't come,' Magda replies and begins to salt the ham that is to be buried with Mamita. She is thinking about her life. Death tells us so much about what it is to live, she thinks. At the moment the little handbells stop ringing.

The silence is terrible. Each daughter struggles with the noise inside her. At last they speak, 'Mamita?'

'Mam-ita?'

Magda has one hand on the ham, the other on her heart. Terese is knotting and unknotting her hair. The bells start to ring again. Both sisters scream. Mamita chuckles to herself and bites into a peach.

'A little something yet Magda?'

'Only the beating of my heart Mamita.' Magda kicks her sandals against the chair. She is thinking, I am as dry as the salt-lakes outside. Who will make me wet in this village? What sort of life is this anyway?

'If you cannot find it in yourself to weep for me Magda, I will have to wrap you in a garb of tears. Perhaps in assuming the external signs of grief the tears will come more easily. The breathless smell of black crêpe will help. And I will die knowing the neighbours have seen you cry for your mother on the hour of her death.'

Magda says nothing. If only you knew Mamita . . . how much I am grieving for my life.

Mamita instructs Terese to remove the mothballs and lavender sachets from their grandmother's trunk and to take out the heavy black bombazine dress inside it. Magda looks at the lustreless sombre garment and laughs. 'It will quench the flames of a hundred candles Mamita.'

3

'But it is your tears that should quench the flames of a hundred candles Magda. That dress is BIG grief. Your grandmother wore it the day her husband died – for the rest of her life. She even worked in the fields in it. Despite the heat.'

Magda knows better. Her grandfather had made his wife weep so much when he was alive, when he died she had no tears left to cry for him. Instead she embroidered little black tears on white handkerchiefs and wore the bombazine dress to appease her guilt. But all she said to her mother was, 'I remember the blood puddings Grandmama made. She said they were the blood puddings of shame.'

'Yes Magda. She had seen her sons massacred in the wars.'

'She told me Mamita, that a woman's lot in life is blood and tears.'

'Dress your sister Terese.'

Terese holds up the dress and smiles apologetically. Magda shrugs and undoes the buttons of her sunflower-yellow dress. She had dreamed of wearing it when she went to university in the city. But dreams are dreams.

'It is always the women who carry the burden of mourning wrappers,' she smiles nastily at Terese who zips and hooks up the black bombazine.

'Watch out, I've got ring worm!' Terese backs away, scared of her disgruntled older sister.

'Yes. There's a worm in this,' Magda slaps her chest. The bombazine is so heavy it sinks her shoulders in an attitude of grief and resignation. It makes her walk slowly and deliberately. Even her sun-browned skin looks white in comparison.

'And the gloves! If you cannot weep for me, your hands will weep for me.' Magda holds out her hands

4

and gives no help to Terese who struggles and tugs at her fingers to get the gloves on.

'And you will wear the jet necklace. Your neck will weep for me too! A string of tears. I cut the stones myself. With a lathe.'

'Black as your teeth Mamita.'

Magda hops uncomfortably from foot to foot like a large black crow.

'How do you feel Magda?'

'Desolate Mamita.'

'Good.'

Mamita sighs and allows herself to enter the pictures in her mind's eye.

An orchard of cherries ripening in the sun.

Magda stares at the vast portrait of her mother, framed in gold and painted in oils (cracked as my lips and spirit she thinks) hanging in the place of honour. Sprouting from Mamita's chin is one long black whisker. Mamita had always called it the Whisker Of Wisdom. She grew it in the most bitter part of her marriage, when she decided she wanted nothing more to do with her husband. Her daughters secretly knew she had grown it to repulse him. At the same time she took to wearing pyjamas when she lay with him, instead of the traditional white cotton nightdress which her mother had given her on her wedding night. The pyjamas, made from thick purple felt, were so sealed and snug he could not slip his hands into them – or anything else for that matter. He called them 'The Purple Pyjamas Of Defiance'. When Mamita decided to sleep alone in the hammock she still wore them. She sweated and itched but it was worth it.

One night, in rage, after he had been particularly humiliated by her scheming to keep him out of her thoughts and body, he crept into her room and plucked the whisker out of her chin. She woke up and howled so loudly, rumour had it wolves prowled the village that night. But Mamita and her family knew better and did not bother to erect wire fences in the yard to protect the chickens.

'I will grow you another whisker, Demon Man,' she had shrieked, but much as she tried, watering her chin with creams and oils and eating particular vegetables, another never grew.

And then there was the time her mother had thumped a gnarled solid lump of wood so hard with her iron-tipped boots it broke into kindling for the fire. Magda remembered the determination, the sheer will in that banging, banging, banging. Magda wakes up because Terese is pulling her arm and there is someone banging on the door.

Mamita lying upstairs knows that three knocks on a door means death is very near. She furiously crams more grapes into her mouth so as to relish the flavour one last time.

'Who is it Terese?'

'José Mamita.'

'Haaaaaaaa Haaaaaaaa! José! My putrescent corpse is your interest-free capital, is that not so José? You have come to collect yet more money for my death plot!' Mamita's brown body shakes with laughter and a flurry of little bells. José smiles, his eyes settling on Terese's breasts.

'Give him the three coins under the vase Terese, and tell him to lower his eyes.'

José shuffles his feet and holds out a tin box which Terese fills with the coins. They fall to the bottom with a hollow clanking sound. His eyes shift from Terese to Magda.

'I see you are in heavy mourning already. You are a dutiful daughter. Perhaps you would make a dutiful wife?' Magda scowls but he continues all the same.

'It is a matter of great sadness in the village, your mother's death. When her hair fell out, a flock of birds fell from the sky. I saw with my own eyes.'

'My mother has all her hair,' Terese whispers, her cheeks filling with colour.

'Is that so little one?' He smiles again, and strokes her cheek with parchment fingers, one nail curiously long, curved and yellow, not unlike a bird's claw. Magda strides to the door and slams it in his face.

'Don't let him in Terese!' Magda shouts fiercely when the door bangs again. Terese thinks how like her mother Magda is getting.

Bang. Bang. Bang.

Mamita wants to shout too but her mouth is full of hot house fruit.

Magda opens the door violently . . .

'Go away you capitalista cockerel! May your private organs blister and pop!'

A woman stands on the doorstep. Her head is a skull draped in yew leaves. She wears a scarlet velvet dress covered in mud and moss.

'Am I too late?' she whispers throatily.

Magda and Terese hold their breath and stare.

'Am I?'

Mamita spits out a mouthful of grape pips and peers through the muslin drapes.

'No you are not you goat turd of a daughter!'

Two surprisingly young and fleshy hands remove the skull, and there in front of them, tears of laughter run-

7

ning down her cheeks, is Rosita. She hugs and kisses her sisters, breaking off bits of the skull and eating it.

'It's sugar! Here. Have some teeth! I have just come from Mexico! I went to a festival for the dead. We danced like this.'

She claps her hands and stamps her feet and dances for her sisters.

'Come up my daughter.'

Rosita skips up the stairs scattering yew leaves and the remainder of the skull's jawbone. She kneels at her mother's side and kisses her hands.

'You have been to the Festival Of The Dead, Rosita?'

'Yes. I danced with the dead! They smelt of nutmeg.'

'Aaaaah. Nutmeg,' Mamita sighs.

'And I have something to tell you.'

'Tell me then my child.'

Rosita fiddles with her dress . . .

'I met papa. We danced together.'

Mamita squeezes her hand in rage.

'I hope you trod hard on his corns.'

'He says Mamita . . . the whisker he plucked out . . .'

Mamita spits and turns her head away.

'He says that whisker has stuck in him like a prickle in a pear. He can't get it out. But he's used to it now. It reminds him of you. He says it's the prickle in his heart.'

Mamita laughs and the bells laugh with her.

'And who else did you dance with?'

'Many of the dead. The leaves crackled under our feet. And then at midnight they planted their feet and turned into trees.'

'But you danced with someone else?'

'No Mamita.' Rosita looks away from her mother whose eyes are wrinkling into two islands of disapproval. Her voice takes on a dangerously familiar gentleness of tone.

'Come closer.'

Rosita moves a little nearer, not unlike a cringing cat.

Her mother grasps hold of her neck and buries her face in it.

'You smell of lemons.'

'I smell of lemons because I squeezed their juice to quench my thirst on the journey.'

Mamita swats a fly that has settled on her cheek. Outside, a donkey yawns.

'After the festival did you hurry home to mourn for your mother?'

'Yes.'

Rosita can feel her sisters listening through the muslin. She can smell Magda light another cheroot. Mamita's voice drops a tone.

'You smell of the church.'

'Yes Mamita. I went to the church to say my last prayers for you.'

'Since when have prayers smelt of lemons?'

Mamita pushes her away so hard she hits her head on the wall.

'You smell of priest! My nose has never misled me. I can smell his beard. Yes. I can smell his hands on your body.'

Magda now surrounded by cheroot smoke guffaws. She looks very impressive striding about in her black bombazine, cheroot dangling from her lips . . .

'So! Our sister has been rolling about in the lemon orchard with that priest who smells of anchovy paste and tooth picks! Ha! I'd rather be the donkey than have that man touch me! What with his sickly sermons and pork fat jokes!'

Terese who is repotting two little cacti merely puts her hands on her belly and weeps. Magda stops her striding and looks long and hard at her distraught sister.

'You too! Our communion angel?' Terese nods her head and her tears water the cacti.

'Well Well. The shepherd flirts with all his ewes!'

'What are you girls whispering about?' Mamita screams.

'Never has a mother had to bear such a burden as these daughters of mine. Go down Rosita. Join your sisters. Good. I like to see you cry. Tears keep a woman out of trouble.'

Rosita walks down the stairs barely able to look her sisters in the eye. Magda breaks the silence by hugging both of them, giving Rosita a puff on her cheroot and pouring each of them a small glass of apricot brandy. They huddle together to hear their mother's last words.

'My daughters. This is my last communion with you all. Death sits on my chest . . .'

'Turn over then Mamita,' shouts back Magda and her sisters try to smother their giggles.

'No. It is better that I lie on my back facing heaven. For life is spilling out of me. I am glad I am not the moon and do not have to be reborn over and over again. One life on earth is enough . . .' She is interrupted by Terese who sneezes three little sneezes.

'You will have triplets Terese,' Magda whispers a little drunkenly.

And then it happens! The daughters of Mamita all start to sneeze. The room fills with quick little sneezes that become so contagious, feverish, glorious, none of them can stop; not even when Mamita shouts in her most steely and forbidding voice.

'I forbid all sneezing. Do you hear? Stop it! Do you

hear? Every time you sneeze a part of your soul escapes, do you hear? There are too many souls for one room.'

'It's ... the ... te ... ten ... tenssssssion ... mam ... choo,' Rosita sneezes wetly, followed by her sisters who stuff their fists into their mouths to try and stop, but all to no avail. The sneezes have to be sneezed.

'Stop it! Stop it! Stop it!' yells Mamita in hysterics. 'Your souls will enter my body and torment my own soul ... cut your noses off rather than sneeze.'

But her daughters continue to sneeze. Solo, in duet, all three at once. There is nothing they can do to stop it. It is as if a lifetime's worth of sneezes are being sneezed and even the sight of Mamita parting the muslin drapes and slashing the air with a knife as she shrieks is not enough to stop them.

'You rotting sticks of liquorice ... you rancid salamis ...' Swish swish as her knife cuts through the muslin ... 'I will plunge this into all of you ... all three of you ... Magda ... Terese ... Ros ... Ros ... Rosiiiiiii ...' Mamita tries to restrain herself. Her will and her body battle with each other. She writhes, bends her knees, clutches her sides and gasps.

'EEEEEEEEEEEEEEEEEEEAAAAAAAACHA AAAAACHAAAAAACHAAAAAAOOOOOOOO.'

Mamita sneezes. The Sneeze Of All Sneezes, the walls shake, the floorboards rattle, all the clay bowls in the house crack, and as her sneeze completes itself, to the horror of all in the room, a little white mouse crawls out of her mouth and scampers about the floor.

Mamita is in convulsions.

'You see! Aiiii Aiiii! My soul has escaped. Find it ... find it my daughters. If the soul escapes before the body is dead it becomes vengeful for it envies the living.'

Whereupon her daughters start the long search for

Mamita's scampering rattling soul. They search under chairs, curtains, in drawers, in the fireplace, to cries of 'Here, it's in the water bucket.' 'No, under the window. Quick!' while Mamita writhes on her bed crying.

'There is nothing for it. You will have to appear to be in a miserable state so it will not envy you, you should be miserable anyway you goat turd daughters.'

The room becomes a museum of pain and gestures; they wring their hands, wail, throw back their heads, fall to their knees, pray, tear at their flesh, until at last, Magda finds the mouse and takes it by the tail to show Mamita.

'You must tie it to my bedpost and feed it every ten minutes. My soul must be made to feel comfortable again after so great a trauma.'

Magda ties the writhing rodent to the bedpost with a turquoise ribbon and orders Terese to slice a little of the ham and put it on a saucer. They listen to it eating. From downstairs they can hear the pitt patt of its spindly feet as it pulls against the ribbon and also the sound of Mamita weeping quietly, little sobs between the sound of her soul guzzling and trying to escape at the same time. The sisters clutch each other and weep too.

'Are you sad Mamita?' Magda's voice is surprisingly tender. She is thinking how strange it is that Mamita's soul should be a little white mouse, all a-quiver and smelling of straw.

'I am thinking I might not take my place with the Saints after all,' Mamita replies in a little sobbing voice.

'Of course you will Mamita. They have swept and cleaned for you.' Magda wipes her eyes on the bombazine sleeve. Terese and Rosita join in.

'They have woven a hammock for you.'

'They are cooking yellow banana and chilli to welcome you darling.'

Mamita continues to sob and her voice gets smaller and smaller.

'I am thinking I did not treat your father as a woman should.'

Magda puts on her fiercest voice, 'The Saints will understand. For haven't they suffered at the hands of men themselves?' She counts on her fingers, 'St Lucy who plucked her eyes out rather than submit to the bishop's lust. St Agatha who had her breasts torn off for similar reasons. St Catherine who had her back broken on the wheel. St Joan whom they burnt before she was fully grown. No Mamita! They will welcome you.'

Mamita seems comforted. Every now and again the sisters take turns to carry up a saucer of ham for the little white mouse soul, who looks happy curled up by Mamita's toes. There is a calm feeling in the house. Mamita speaks very gently into the silence and dripping candles.

'Magda. You will go to the university. I have arranged this for you. My eldest daughter who makes thoughts so sharp they line her forehead. Study hard and don't smoke too much.'

Magda throws back her head and lets out a long happy sigh. She will carry a leather case full of books and cheroots, okay, only one packet of cheroots for when she has to write essays.

'Mamita. Thank you.'

'Terese. I have noticed you are good at making things grow. You like working on the land?'

'Oh yes Mamita.'

'I have talked with Pepe. He is a good kind man. He

will teach you everything he knows and has worked on the land all his life. You will look after my orchards, olive and lime, my grazing land and the three donkeys. They are yours.'

Terese laughs happily. She will soon have a baby to play with too. Another body to work with her outside. She will ask her friend, the old spinster Inez, to help look after it.

'There is nothing that would make me happier Mamita.'

'Rosita. I have arranged for that priest to be removed to another parish. He has not sufficient brain to be worthy of my daughter.'

Magda catches Terese's eye. But Terese just shrugs. She is trying to think of a way to irrigate the orchards all year round.

'It seems to me Rosita, you have a liking for spectacle, festivals, dresses of scarlet velveteen, masks and dance. You must make your own travelling theatre company with people from the village around here. You will name it after me and make great celebrations. I have left you three barns in which to meet, your Grandmamita's violin and guitar, and a little money.'

'Thank you! I will sweep out the barn facing south because it has the best light and we will have our first meeting tomorrow.'

Mamita seems to be rambling now. She mutters something about tasting sangria in her mouth and it seems that she has summoned a lover from the past who is kissing her breasts, who is kissing her somewhere nice for she Ah's and Coo's and Sighs until the bells stop ringing. Completely stop. Mamita has died exactly at the hour she predicted and in a state of orgasmic bliss.

Her daughters quickly and efficiently perform all rituals that will ensure their mother a good send-off to take her place with the Saints. They shake out pillows containing feather of dove, veil pictures and mirrors, inform all the domestic animals they own, including the bees, that Mamita is now dead, open all locks and loosen the knots in the carpet. Then they walk arm in arm to the river, undress and plunge into the icy water.

Mamita's soul has by now gnawed its way through the turquoise ribbon and scampered across the parched fields. It runs to a tree and watches the women swim in the water, naked and wet and glistening in the sun. Satisfied, it leaves them and plays in the long white grass with butterflies and clover flowers, well fed, free and in the fresh air, thinking this is life just how it should be.

THE SINFUL TWINS

WHEN CONNIE WAS young and her body her wealth, she starred in a pornie movie called 'The Sinful Twins'. She bought a villa in Spain with the money she earned (her first independent income) and the projectionist congratulated her on her performance. She still has his phone number scrawled in her scarlet leather diary on which lingers the old-time perfume of gin, French scent and tobacco.

She met Owen when they were both making a B-movie in Cairo. Back in England she had forty fiancés, sixteen of them Tory MPs willing to risk marrying a porno queen despite possible smear campaigns, but it was Owen who won her heart and they moved to Paris during the war where they lived in splendour on the black market. Owen came from Cork and was really an artist, but his handsome Irish bones and droll way of delivering badly written lines got him bit-parts in movies. With this money he bought paints and canvas and the occasional bow tie. Connie, a slim blonde with eyes like raisins and a crooked winning smile, had a kind of excitement locked in her long lithe limbs that made her an energetic proposition.

In Paris they drank and smoked themselves into faint-

ing fits – they took it in turns, contemplated joint sui-
cides on the Métro when adrenalin was low, always
had butter on their table (an untold luxury that re-
presented a corrupt deal of one kind or another), ate
eagle flesh and dove omelettes. When food was particularly scarce they ate horse steaks, Owen said the jockey
would have been more tender, and once, but only once,
American tinned meat. Both agreed this was uncouth
and inelegant and no matter how hungry would never
touch the stuff again. Returning to their room in the
early hours, Owen would take his easel out on to the
balcony and paint the balmy light while Connie decorated her gas mask with blue and white polka dots to
match her party dress. Their greatest fear (and they lived
in fearful times) was silence; they were often relieved to
hear the air-raid sirens. When Connie could not sleep
she would take out her tarot cards and lay them on
Owen's sleeping buttocks. She only told him the good
news and hid the fact that death placed itself on his left
buttock on at least three occasions.

Owen says he went to fight in Spain but can't remember exactly when. It was during The Civil War, and for
the Republicans, because he preferred their black berets
to the khaki of the Fascists. When he arrived the revolution was all but lost, the anarchist flags taken down
and a republic gone down in blood with it, so to console
himself he set up 'housekeeping' with a peachskinned
Spanish virgin, famous for her lustrous coil of black
hair, whom he devoured and deflowered with all the
passion of his vermilion tube of paint. Recognising a
potential money-spinner, he began to sketch famous
people drifting in and out of Spain at the time; Ernest
Hemingway cutting off a bull's ear, his right arm (his
writing arm) streaked with blood; Lillian Hellman writ-

ing a letter to Hammett in a café that stank of rancid olive oil; George Orwell searching for a cigarette end on the floor of a bar in Catalonia; Auden and MacNeice throwing pennies into a muddy pool somewhere in Madrid; Marya Levy giving broadcasts in her yiddish accent, her earrings glistening bait for the fat flies who buzzed around her coiffured head; Spender and Isherwood standing by the broken torso of a bombed statue. These pictures, some of them water-colour, others, quick sketches, were later sold at exorbitant prices to publishers, art collectors and galleries. He also met artists who risked imprisonment under Franco for recording the truth in their paintings. Owen promised to smuggle their work out of Spain (he was to collect many 'dissident' paintings in the same manner throughout his lifetime) and return them when times were less harsh. This never happened, partly because there was a fire in his Kensington studio, and partly because he sold them, believing the artists to be dead or rotting in gaol. As well as the luscious virgin and countless paintings that were to become very valuable, he picked up a smattering of languages, phrases, jokes, and used them through the years to show he was a well-travelled man.

What Connie did during this time we don't know. It is rumoured she was seen floating paper boats down the Seine and graffiting the windscreens of cars with lipstick. In fact she smuggled a whole box-load of lipsticks back to England and got through customs by convincing the officials they were suppositories.

After the war Connie and Owen moved into a studio in Kensington. Owen devoted all his time to painting and was slowly becoming famous. Connie modelled for him (he always painted her as a kind of chaste femme fatale, exaggerating her crooked mouth and cleavage), administered for him, entertained and delighted his business associates and artist friends. She was fond of telling them how much she despised intellectual men because their self-discipline made them impotent, and in her experience it was only when they were ill and delirious with fever that they allowed suppressed feeling and impulse to overrule their brain. The intellectuals among them sipped their wine and resolved to spend less time reading in bed at night. Sometimes if she was in a good mood she would give them kissing lessons in the hallway, saying things like, 'Don't kiss me like a full stop. I want a semicolon . . . a dot dot dot . . .' at which point Max Bloch, who was a willing pupil, squeezed her harder and said, 'Dots amazing, show me just vonce more . . .'

Owen, brought up a Catholic, now resumed the faith and went to Mass every Sunday. This dialogue with religion began to reflect itself in his paintings which, like Rodin's marbles, were more sentimental than erotic, lacking the urgency of passion. Connie never said much about his work, but on her own would stare at it for hours; apart from one picture of herself as a pregnant angel peeling potatoes in heaven, she missed the lateral whimsy of his earlier paintings and, indeed, of his kisses.

One night he placed two candles at the top and bottom of their bed and somehow managed to make it look like an altar. While they were making love he insisted that she stop contracepting herself. She slunk out of bed and went to get herself a cold beer, resenting the fact that God had become a voyeur between them.

'Where exactly is your God, Owen?'

'I think, sweetheart, God lies under my tongue . . . just here . . .'

Connie, then and there, resolved to bite G.O.D. out

of him. It was a bloody decision and afterwards Owen was unable to eat anything hot for a week. Soon after this incident she fell pregnant with her first and only daughter who will later become an avant-garde feminist film maker.

In the first month of her pregnancy Connie planted a bed of radishes (she asked Owen to pray for them), in the second month, a herb-garden, and then she suddenly started to write. She was very happy scribbling away in a private part of the studio and a play began to emerge, slowly taking shape day by day just as her radishes were slowly rooting themselves and beginning to sprout, day by day. Owen was proud of her and told all his friends Connie had 'a good ear for dialogue', but all the same would absent-mindedly clean his brushes with the odd sheet of paper she left exposed by his easel. She said nothing about her work being sabotaged in this manner, merely took to hiding papers under their bed where used condoms, from the days of contraception, and salmon pieces from feasts in bed, congregated in a private mass of their own.

Owen stopped painting and began to hit the bottle. Money was scarce and he thought it time Connie made another pornie movie. She agreed and he contacted Edwardo, an old-time crook and friend who set up a deal with a company in Sweden. Meanwhile, Owen consulted 'gentlemen lawyers' just in case his wife was not paid her full due. Connie sent him three postcards saying she was having a marvellous time; all she had to do was dress up in a black lace nightdress with leather thongs tied to her nipples, and whip the clients who visited her parlour. Although she was feeling sick in the mornings and had lost the urge to smoke, her pregnancy was barely visible. Sweden was cold but there were plenty of people to keep her warm and make a fuss over her. Owen grew insanely jealous and begged her to come home. She arrived seven months later, heavily pregnant, very rich and looking wonderful. Owen laid his ear to her belly and swore no man would touch her again. The child was now kicking hard.

Having recovered from his drinking bout, Owen returned to painting and to Catholicism (the truth was that Connie preferred him taking up alcohol to God) and demanded their child, when born, take up the faith. Obsessed and in love with her pregnant belly, he painted her whenever she was still enough and tired enough not to object. He painted her pregnant in the bath, her long legs wrapped around the taps, pregnant in the garden planting tulip bulbs, asleep and flushed on the rug by the fire. These paintings were to become his most famous, perhaps because the brush strokes were emotional in a way his earlier paintings of her as a femme fatale were only physical, but they mark a change in his work that shows a glimmer of the great artist he could have been. They also mark a change in Connie. For once her body was making demands of its own, rather than other people making demands of it. She complained bitterly about these paintings of herself, especially the one in the bath where she was large and naked and vulnerable. Owen mocked her for this apparently new modesty, saying half the world had seen her naked and she had never objected before. She cried insisting it was not the same and begged him to retrieve that particular painting from a national gallery in Holland. He refused and she never let him paint her again.

Two months after their daughter Cassandra was born Owen packed his pigskin suitcase and left for Hungary, Rome and the USA where he was something of a celebrity and was to be interviewed for television and radio. Connie bought herself a sleek black cat and called it Joe. One morning while Cassandra was asleep guarded by Joe who had fallen in love with the baby girl, she took her old typewriter apart, cleaned its dusty insides with Owen's toothbrush, bought a new ribbon, put it together again and started to rewrite her play. She worked and drank solidly for the two years he was away. The studio in Kensington was littered with Scotch bottles and the cat's ribs stuck out as much as Connie's for lack of food. Only Cassandra flourished. She played alone and shared her milk with Joe whose rough pink tongue lapped up her offerings without guilt. The first word the child said was not M.A.M.A. or P.A.P.A. but J.O.E., while the named creature danced wild circles around her to celebrate the small advance in her evolution; Connie was too drunk to notice. The play now finished (she called it *Crash*) was put on by a small but prestigious theatre company in the North of England. Cassandra accompanied her mother to rehearsals and played with the props in the dressing-room, while her mother, relaxed and happy, realised for the first time in her life that she had ideas to contribute to other people's lives.

Owen returned and accused Connie of entertaining other men while he was away. She denied this, storming out of the house and into the park where she flung herself against a tree. Its bark was carved with a scratchy heart pierced with 'I luv you for ever and ever.' She cried bitterly. Owen ran after her waving his toothbrush in his hand, proof, he said, of her 'extra curricular activities'. On her way home, Connie went into the discount shop and bought two glasses. One marked 'strychnine', the other 'arsenic'.

Once more administering for Owen and entertaining his friends with quips and stories about their life in the war and her life posing for flesh merchants, as she now called them, Connie gave up writing. Owen told stories about temperamental Hungarian mistresses, and about his childhood friend Solly Muggenheim who made a jockstrap out of a squirrel's tail and died in the arms of his 'loverbird', Connie adding that the 'loverbird' told her Solly kissed like a vacuum cleaner. Their daughter played with Joe in her bedroom which Connie had painted sunflower yellow. Her young body was covered with flea bites which she delighted in scratching until they bled and Joe licked clean with his ever obliging tongue.

How their studio in Kensington burnt down remains a mystery, although Connie was convinced that Cassandra set it ablaze; something she never told Owen. The only clue to this was that one night when she was taking the child's shoes off, she noticed the rubber soles were melted and the little girl's hands covered in blisters – which suggested she might have been playing with matches. When questioned, Cassandra pointed to Joe who was sitting by the window, watching city birds with his brooding yellow eyes.

Most of the dissident work Owen had been 'keeping' for the respective artists was frazzled in this fire or in the flames of Cassandra's revenge or in the flames of Joe's eyes. The paintings were conceived, so to speak, in fire, and ended in fire; had they survived and been redistributed to the artists who had sweated over them, perhaps at least one of them, now living 'underground' in Poland, would, at the grand old age of sixty-nine, have been able to live the rest of his days in some degree

24

of comfort and security. As it was, he died of bronchitis, poverty and lack of recognition.

With the money they got from the insurance, they decided to buy a ruin in the East End of London and turn it into a 'cream-cake'. The walls were covered in Italian hand-rolled marbled wall-paper, the floors in black Italian tiles, the ceiling painted by a famous Hungarian artist who accepted a crate of vintage wine as his fee, and every room in the house was photographed by international interior designers. By the fifth year an aviary was constructed and exotic birds were flown in from all over the world, and by the seventh, an orchard of dwarf orange trees lined the hallway. Tycoon friends from America filled their fridge with champagne, the sponsors of one of Owen's exhibitions in Athens, a Greek shipping firm, sent them a crate of prawns and squid, and, not to be outdone, a Chinese maestro sent them a large flattened duck. The house, their first project together since making the bad movie in Cairo all those years ago, amused and absorbed them. By the eighth year (which seemed like no time at all) they both had a bad case of DT's, were utterly broke, had nothing to say to each other, and Owen had taken up religion again.

Shifting the rosary beads between finger and thumb as he shifted his bleary thoughts, Owen hit on an idea for making vast sums of money just as the collection tin arrived at his pew. Why didn't he and Connie take themselves to tea at a place like the Ritz or the Savoy, keep a discreet eye on who came in and when they departed, watch the chauffeur put them in the car (preferably a Daimler or a Mercedes) and he, Owen, would step in front of the car (timing was everything), get run over, while Connie could be witness and they could sue for thousands of pounds compensation. Connie thought it 'an almond of an idea' and bought herself a black dress edged with grey sable to match her shoe buckles. The bank manager even gave them a generous overdraft facility on the understanding that money was coming in soon. Owen chose his underwear very carefully and eventually decided on purple. Connie told him the doctor would think he was a cardinal's son.

They had a fragile pink salmon tea and Owen kissed all the waitresses' hands. A portly middle-aged gentleman and his wife left the hotel and were observed being ushered into their car by a very bored chauffeur. Connie and Owen paid their bill and involved themselves in a conversation on the pavement. Owen crossed the road – the one thing he had learnt from his stint in B-movies was timing – and was promptly run over. He was rushed to hospital suffering from a splintered hip, sprained ankle and a cut on his forehead that needed five stitches. The chauffeur was killed; Connie and Owen won eighty-five thousand pounds compensation. Cards arrived from all over the world wishing Owen better; the hotel sent them a bottle of malt whisky with 'deepest regrets' and Mrs B. across the road waited for her Giro to arrive so she could make him a nourishing broth to sip in bed. When he was feeling a little stronger he went to physiotherapy for his hip and damaged left leg. Cassandra, now nine years old, regretted not being able to go for walks with her father, even when his hip was repaired he still limped and had to stop every few yards. Connie often took her to the movies and then for a sickly treat somewhere. For her tenth birthday Cassandra was given a camera and went walking on her own through the dead docklands, eating peanuts and taking pictures.

Thirteen years later Connie decided to have plastic surgery. Her stomach was wrinkled and she wanted it firmed up. Owen agreed it would be a shame for her otherwise impeccable figure to be ruined by the cruelty of passing years and they used the very last of their money to pay for the operation. When Connie returned, her newly flattened belly wrapped in bandages, she found Owen on the floor in a drunken stupor, muttering something about being the true landlord of County Clare. He demanded the deeds be dug up and given back to their rightful owner – after all he was a man of the land and it had been the inspiration of many of his paintings. From then on he refused to work, not only to paint, but also to do the odd bit of journalism for art magazines that had kept them going when the icing on their 'cream-cake' wore thin. Connie tried to write again but her scars were more painful than she expected and she was out of practice. She lamented the fact that she was too old to do another pornie movie, and that Owen spent most of his time in prayer, demanding justice from his birth land. Cassandra, who was now a star student at an eminent film school, lent them a fiver from her grant whenever she could and always bought them a packet of gammon steaks which were their favourite – although they told friends they had to eat couscous at least twice a week or they would die. When Cassandra left the house, the apparently immortal Joe who had not aged at all, made strange crooning noises in his throat, spine arched with a private grief of his own.

It was while grilling the sizzling flesh of the gammon steaks that Owen hit on another idea for making money. As the scars from Connie's surgery were taking so long to heal, why didn't she deliberately infect them and sue

27

the surgeon for negligence? Connie thought it a great idea and set about infecting her wounds. When the pain got too bad Owen would numb her with whisky. They lodged their complaint, threatened to inform the press, and without it even going to court were given sixty thousand pounds by the Harley Street surgeon to take the matter no further. The pain often made Connie feel nauseous and feverish, but she rubbed vitamin E oil into the scars every night and every morning. Cassandra, worried by her shivering pale mother, suggested she should go to her villa in Spain and recuperate in the sun.

Owen stayed at home and entertained a young woman who was rather intrigued by his silver hair, bow ties, perfect gestures, wit and endless amusing stories. Every time she offered him one of her cigars he'd kiss her hand and say, 'oh you're sweet'. One night he cried into his canary silk handkerchief and then on the shoulder of her leather jacket and told her about a nun he had known as a young man in Cork. Apparently she had set up a rehabilitation centre for 'alcoholics and sexpots'. The woman wondered which of the two he might have been, but allowed the thought to go no further, merely parted her glossed lips into a surprised and confession-taunting expression. Apparently this nun had a phenomenal success rate because she cured people not through 'imposition' but through 'implication'. Joe screwed his eyes into little yellow slits, allowing them to settle on a pile of bloody steak in the kitchen. Owen's lady-friend had bought it for his dinner and was going to cook it for him in the special way her mother cooked it for her father.

Cassandra invited her father to the preview of her first film entitled *Catholic Frolics*. Connie had already sent her a good luck telegram apologising for her absence on such an important occasion, but said she was very proud and loved the title. Owen met his daughter in the foyer and was given a complimentary ticket embroidered with a bleeding heart. He was concerned to feel his own heart beating hard against his shirt, a sensation he had not experienced for years and now found oddly disturbing. A poster was being unravelled and a crowd of people shrieking with laughter were gathered around it.

RECONSTRUCTED SALUTES AND DEDICATIONS
EXPANDED POETICS
THE BODY OF CHRIST WITH THE SOUL OF LENIN
CHRIST DRAGGED SCREAMING INTO HEAVEN BY
PRESS-GANG ANGELS

He limped to his seat and fumbled for a cigarette.

'God bless us.'
'Dress us.'
'Depress us.'
'Regress us.'
'Digress us.'

A pregnant nun and a half-dressed man sit at an elaborately laid table, heads bowed, eerie shadows flickering over their faces in the candle light as they bless themselves. This ritual over, they pick up a polished silver fork and plunge the prongs into the palms of their hands. Stigmata now achieved, they pour themselves out a bloody Mary and talk about the riot police who have invaded every large city and even some rural villages. Every now and again the man gets up from the table and walks to the coal fire where two kebabs cook on the flames.

The kebab meat, which is lamb, is skewered to sticks shaped like crucifixes, and referred to as Christ Kebabs. The nun suddenly gets labour pains and is helped to the fire where she lies down and screams the names of saints, political leaders and frozen food products. She lifts the folds of her habit to reveal a red satin lining decorated with a hammer and sickle and begins to push while the man sings the *Internationale* to the tune of *The Lord's My Shepherd*. She gives birth, at last, to a moonfaced, black-haired baby girl with golden skin and slanting eyes. When the baby cries, her tears are rice grains and trickle into the small sad piles on the floor.

Much later, Owen told Connie that when he staggered out of the cinema half way through the film, distraught and sweating, all he could see was his now deceased grandmother pouring scalding wax over his bare toes as a young boy to give him an impression of the horrors of hell. He limped home and watered his tomato plants with fearful trembling hands. It will be two years before he speaks to Cassandra again by which time it is she who refuses to talk to him. The plants died two days later.

Connie returned from Spain tanned, healthy and fully recovered from the pain and pus of her infected scars. Owen counted her mosquito bites, eighty-one in all, and they both agreed he never got bitten because he had bad blood. She told him about a woman she'd met in Spain; a woman with a long lustrous coil of black-going-silver hair, and a daughter, a painter of great imagination and technique, now exhibiting all over Barcelona. This was a great comfort to her mother who had apparently met a young Irish man during The Civil War and been abandoned when she fell pregnant. Chastised for her unmarried pregnancy, she was thrown out of the house by her brothers and father, who only a few months earlier had called her comrade, and had taken in washing to keep herself going. Under the lime tree the woman had said to Connie, 'If only men knew how many sons and daughters they had scattered around the shores of the world, they would look at every child, and later, every adult, with morbid curiosity'. She and Connie became great friends, walking together, swimming, cooking, but mostly just talking together. The best place to talk was always under the lime tree, and it was there, late one afternoon after a lazy lunch, that the daughter had painted them both. It was the first painting of herself that Connie ever liked, the composition of her face and body in relation to another, a thinking body and face painted by a hand that wanted to record and celebrate a historic turn of events. Owen said it was a sweet story and rubbed some calamine lotion on Connie's mosquito bites. He made her promise never to leave him alone again.

Dirt Dirt Dirt Dirt Dirt Dirt Dirt Dirt Dirt Dirt is the title of Cassandra's third film looking at women and pornography. The title attracted as many men as it did women. They queued up outside the cinema, casting quick clandestine glances at the Sex Queen poster, a voluptuous red-head breast-feeding the Chief of Police, the Minister of Defence, a stockbrocker and an Inspector of Taxes. Perhaps all those months in her mother's belly when the nipple that was later to feed her had been tied with leather thongs and used to beat clients in the parlour of a porn movie set, or perhaps the camera's heat burning through the black-laced five-month swelling of her actress mama's belly had sown the seeds of dissent into the seed. Cassandra invites her mother to see the film. Connie wore the dress her Spanish friend had made for her and bleached her hair for the occasion. She kissed her daughter excitedly, leaving little imprints of her scarlet Cupid lips on Cassandra's cheeks and looked almost as furtive as some of the audience who met her glance with a kind of familiarity that frightened them both. In the dark of the auditorium, a box of popcorn on her lap, she cried great noisy elephant tears that started in the pit of her stomach, crept up to her chest, flooded out of her eyes and soaked her new dress. To her embarrassment they wouldn't stop themselves and she had to creep up the aisle, scattering popcorn everywhere, to the Ladies Room where she could let the cry complete itself and then touch up her make up. Afterwards she is taken out to dinner by Cassandra and her film friends, and tries, in between the avocado and the red mullet, to understand her disquiet.

Connie returned home to find Owen immersed in a painting of Joe. He had tied the cat to the straw chair and placed a perfect Spanish honeydew melon by Joe's feet to bring out the amazing colour of his eyes. Joe was struggling with the cords trying to bite through them with his sharp pointed teeth, arching his back and making fearful noises in his throat. Perhaps it was not just the cords that made Joe jerk his head from side to side so desperately, but the thought of his spirit (which was, after all, an immortal spirit) being sapped; something being taken away from him in the act of reproducing his image. When Owen who seemed for the first time in years excited by what his hands were doing, limped into his studio to find a particular tube of black paint, Connie untied the cords and Joe leapt off the chair banging his tail with great thuds on the floor. Furious at being interrupted just when he was feeling alive and inspired again, Owen broke the straw chair and sat in a corner all evening drinking a bottle of Scotch. He finished off with three glasses of green Chartreuse (in the glass marked strychnine) in tribute to the monks and their secret recipe in the parched hills of Chartreuse.

In the early hours of the morning, Connie woke with something of the old excitement seeping back into her long limbs. Joe sat on the edge of the bed purring a resonant purr, but apart from that she seemed to have woken up to something she described later as 'an atmosphere'. She got out of bed, careful not to disturb Owen, and opened the window, always a shocking experience given that what lay outside the 'cream-cake' was in stark contrast to the opulence within. The pavement lined with grimy struggling trees, rubbish and broken glass, the battered cars parked askew, all seemed extra shocking this particular morning. The blonde hairs on her arm were standing on end. And then she realised, not realised, knew, partly because her body had given her clues, that Owen was not breathing. Imagining a camera was following her, she slowly walked to his side of the bed, the only sound in the room being the pad pad of her feet on the carpet and Joe's steady purr. He was lying on his back as he always did, his arms folded on his chest as they always were, but on his forehead, eyes, nose and mouth, four ebony cat hairs fluttered gently from the draught of the window. A little pile of cat fluff nested in the cleft of his chin. And Owen wasn't breathing.

Joe has his eyes shut tight. He knows he is being observed and prefers the images behind his eyes.

Connie is wondering at this moment, her toes curling inside her leopard-skin slippers, whether an incident is called 'death by misadventure' or 'death by natural causes' if a beast took it upon himself to sit on the head of a sleeping man, and the head was too full of alcohol and God and Hell to notice. She reaches for the bottle of vitamin E oil and rubs it into the creases of her belly. Then she brushes her hair until all the tangles of the night are out, files a jagged nail on her left hand, looks for her scarlet leather diary and phones her daughter to find out what to do.

PROLETARIAN ZEN

HOW ZEN MASTER change sister life?

First sister play many hour with silkworm. She wash
saké cup when saké cup clean. She arrange flower till
flower open mouth lose youth. She become very strict
housekeeper. Every day she make health food. Other
sister feel pale moon so much health food. Today she
make beancurd seaweed carrot small portion rice. Take
to sister in garden. She give each chopstick tell chew
very slow. First sister often get migraine. She lie on
futon dim light, try make sense disturbance behind eye
and in heart. She image hand of Zen master place lightly
small of back. This make feel better. Sometime she read
book increase understanding of life.
             Book often confuse sister.

Second sister no like beancurd. She image prawnburger
and Cola. This sister modern. In morning she buy roller-
skate at market, tuck dress in knicker practise motion
on wheel, concentrate keep weight forward; haiku make
itself. She careful not scuff knee. Zen master no like
scab knee he want woman smooth like melon. Second
sister write many poem. She read at small gathering to

Very Big clap. Zen master approve. Sometime he slip holy arm in sister arm walk across flat grass where she speak new idea. He like sister be excited. In head. But sister also get excited in flesh. When this happen master make cold eye, give sister koan solve.

Sister write very sad poem.

Third sister like beancurd very much. She eat all second sister beancurd. She have many chin. On ear very many jewel, see no ear only jewel. Black eye much fire. Third sister dream of Zen mistress all Sun all Moon. She want put jewel ear on dark belly Zen mistress listen woman secret. Zen mistress very secret woman. She crush lemon verbena leaf on skin. Third sister intoxicate. She eat way through thousand plan catch heart Zen mistress.

New chin grow. New jewel on ear.

Under lemon tree Zen master and first sister make love. It happen once month because Zen master swear celibacy vow. He break vow but jade stem need friend. It citrus affair. He silent. She satisfy. After, drink lemon kill thirst.

Much juice.

Second sister smell Zen sex on first sister and write more sad poem. Rainstorm run down cheek. Why why why why why why second sister want know, Zen master choose illiterate one? Such clever man. Why he choose one with evil headache, who measure bowel movement in morning, check tongue for white sickness, who think haiku mean sound cock crow? Why not she with almond eye, shoulder like dancer? She ask him. Yes. Fed up. She make contraceptive. Very clever. From lychee skin. Aaaah.

36

She want taste Zen master.

'Thigh glorious plump,' whisper Zen mistress in jewel ear third Zuki sister.

'Body smell make deeelirious.' Third sister take red pearl from ear thread pubic hair Zen mistress.

'We meet often?' Zen mistress moan.

'Often.'

Under lime nylon duvet swap story and sister introduce

Zen mistress pork scratching and beer.

'Pig wonderful beast,' Zen mistress say, mouth full.

'Woman more wonderful.'

Third sister switch on TV. Watch election result.

'We see nation massacre itself,' Zen mistress sigh.

Advert come. Many kiss.

Zen master drink wine with disciple in garden many stone. Wrist quiet for Sundown teaching. He smoke thin cigarette. New gold ring on finger. He make loud laugh. Second Zuki sister hear before see. Colour fry in cheek. She curse body telltale. 'I GLIDE TO HIM,' she say. Curious beetle watch. She glide to him. She arrive. She sit very close. Zen disciple disappear. Master lift eye-brow high on holy forehead. Curious beetle turn on back.

Sister improvise scenario.

First Zuki sister lie on hard floorboard. She exercise weak muscle small of back. Breathe in deep hold, lift leg breath out, lower leg back hard floorboard. She make note go dentist next rice harvest. She feel good humour. Why? No tell why!

She decide prepare small treat for sister.

'What can do for second sister?' ask Zen master.
  'I want speak with you.'
  'Speak.' He make magnificent gesture.
  'I would like offer non-literary experience.'
  'Ah.' Zen master put hand to lip. He make thinking sculpture.
  Then he say, 'You offer buy me sweet plum wine?'
  'I do not.'
  'What then might you offer me?' he smile. Second sister say no word.
  'You will sing for me?'
  'I will not.'
  'ENLIGHTEN ME.' He cross arm and wait.
  'I would like fuck with you.' Sister cheek go berserk. She wait answer. Will he give riddle first to solve?
  'Where?'
  Sister surprise. Master answer very quick.
  'Perhaps in car park? Cloud very discreet tonight.'
  Zen master stand up.
  'Come on then,' he say.
  They walk. No look each other. Straight ahead.
  'You very forward woman.' Master catch moth.
  'I no cherry petal exotic.'
  Master laugh and squash moth.

First Zuki sister put three plum in bowl soak maple syrup. Then she wash hand open newspaper election result. It very bloody massacre. Ballot-box full 40% poison. 'Good evening sister,' third sister say. She smell of beer. Eye shine like new computer. She put hand in bowl, take out plum, put in mouth. Lick finger.

38

'Beautiful first sister. I will give massage and then you grow supple like plum tree.'

She stretch out arm. Yawn very deep.

'You drink too much grain liquid to forget massacre?'

First sister put lid on bowl plum. Third sister shake chin.

'You choose new jewel for ear?'

'I commune with Goddess.'

First sister find life very big puzzle.

Door open. Second sister enter. Hair hang like oil rag.

First sister smile Buddha smile.

'Good evening second sister. You mend third sister motor-bike?'

'No.' Second sister sit. She have grease on leg.

Third sister know answer.

'You put oil on body forget massacre?'

'No.' Second sister light small pipe make smoke.

'What then you do?' first sister dare ask, in case sister talk long long time about poem she write.

'I commune with Mini Metro.' Sister make more smoke.

First sister think, aaah sister artist, she make word with spirit of ancestor.

Third sister understand too. Zen mistress tell many tale jade stem in car park.

'Then I must give you massage also.
Make much lead poison come out body.'

First sister despair life pass her by like small butterfly.

Outside bird cry. Footstep in garden. Close. Twig snap. Zen master stand by window. Shadow make two Zen master. First and second sister look each other. Heart flutter like calculator go wrong. Third sister take more plum. Open newspaper on Woman page. Wind blow. Blossom fall soft drift on master. First sister open window. Vein in long neck throb like baby thunder. Zen master speak.

'Like petal scatter in wind
I also make journey.'
    'You leave us master?' Second sister hold breath.
    'They call me back Tokyo.' Zen master wear new straw sandal.
    'You make new temple?' First sister touch pulse.
    'One way yes other way no.'
    Third sister spit out plum stone.
    'You take wife?'
    Master walk two hard footstep. Worm break on grass.
    'No. YOU take wife.' Master close hand. 'I have gift.'
    Master open hand. Red Pearl centre of lifeline.
    'Take.'
    Third sister take. She smile New Moon smile. Put red pearl in mouth. First and second sister no understand.
    Why master give sister gift?
    'What do you do Tokyo?' second sister ask. Already she make sad poem.
    'Now we hear election result it very good time for all master.
They make me manager big car factory.'
    'You Zen capitalist,' third sister scoff.
    Master blink.
    First sister take bowl plum.
    'Master like sweet plum?' she say make voice like lute.
    'I like very much,' master bow head.
    First sister open lid. No plum. She choke dragon.

'I grow plum so I eat plum.' Third sister put out fire.
She look master very fierce eye.

'Master no make car so why master make much gold
lotus?'

Master make wind with hand.

'First sister. You already have small gift from master.'

First sister drop head. Tear fall on kimono.

Second and third sister feel much pain hit breast. Third
sister wipe away tear with chin. Second sister stroke
first sister hair. She feel much noise in sister head.

'Second sister.' Master voice like emperor now he
manager big car factory.

'You speak me master?'

'Second sister. It true you no cherry petal exotic.
Lychee skin like razor. It take off skin jade stem. But
master forgive.'

Second sister make two strawberry in cheek. Master
speak more.

'Zen is radical philosophy. Church of England no
make woman priest. I make you mistress to disciple
here.'

Second sister forget sad poem. She feel light bulb in
chest.

On off on off on off.

'It very great medal master.'

Master click tongue.

'First task. Burn one perfume. Then two perfume.
Then three perfume. Disciple must say what material
go into perfume and write apposite poem. What aim of
task sister?'

Sister think three second.

'Aim of task understand civilisation master.'

'WRONG second sister. Aim of task banish intellect.'

Master make three bow. He have much little white snow in hair. Take five step back, make more bow, turn half moon, leave sister

For Ever.

Second and third sister look at first sister. Sun dip in cloud. Concorde aeroplane fly above house.

'What your gift first sister?'

First sister make no speak. She put hand on belly make

Much Weeping.

Four year pass. Very hard year. New government commit much poverty.

Second sister sit in garden of many stone. She smoke small pipe make much subversive smoke. She famous teacher. In beginning sister find no intellect with disciple to banish. She teach complete work Mao Tse-tung, Marx, Lenin, Alexandra Kollontai, Rosa Luxemburg. Three disciple become barefoot doctor. New government censor sister poem. Italy like sister poem very much. Peasant and worker take turn read. Whole family listen and nod head.

First sister enter garden with young daughter. Often second sister teach first sister and now sister find life not so big puzzle and teach small daughter. Small sister wave Auntie, small hand much love.

'We go roller-skate?'

Sister look each other.

'I do lesson solo,' first sister say. She glad have break. Head full ant. When she say this second sister, sister say not ant, dialectic.

'We go right now.'

They go. Big hand in small hand. Young daughter will scuff knee many many time.

Sound of motor-bike in garden. Snail tuck head in shell.

Third sister speak through helmet. She have four new chin.

'Dearest first sister. I must go give
speech for new election victory. On
new mountain we sing new song.'
She rev motor-bike.
'Are you scare sister?'
'Only seventh chin scare. For what
scientific never fear criticism.'
First sister feel much proud.
'We grow ourself new orchard sister.'
Tree in garden listen. It resolve grow two inch.
'I have message. Zen mistress
make seaweed chestnut duck prawn
thick noodle beancurd beef and rice.
She use whole month social security
cheque. So when you and sister and
small sister want eat, you come.'
First sister no longer get migraine.
'Tell Zen mistress we thank her.
And tell Zen mistress tonight I
oil and coil long black hair
make perfect. We eat soon.'
'Righteo.'

Third sister whizz off. Snail come out shell. Motor-bike have sticker say 'BIG SISTER HAVE BIG VISION'.

Cricket make song in grass. Sky make blush. Tree try very hard grow centimetre. Sound of roller-skate far distance. Blossom make radical juice. First sister shut eyelid. Make very quiet in centre of belly. She think of

43

holiday for daughter sister and Zen mistress. Plan make itself.

Package Tour, Five, Moscow.

END
IS
BEGINNING.

OPHELIA AND THE GREAT IDEA

BEFORE I DIED, why couldn't the man who interviewed me have asked, 'Who do you love, what do you need, what makes you happy/unhappy, what do you like to eat?' Instead, he asked me how much I earned, how much was I likely to earn, where I was educated, how many cars, mistresses and houses I owned.

I wanted to tell him that I had a lovely wife and two lovely daughters. In fact she is my second wife (the first died of the plague) and therefore my second daughter, my wife's first child, is my stepdaughter. I wanted to tell him that this daughter suicided herself, and that my second wife came up to me one day with all her intelligence, wit and beauty, to tell me in the gentlest of tones that she had no choice but to kill her love for me. That we sat together by the lake, both as sad as each other. She asked me about my first wife. I told her that we had a sort of medieval love; remote, unwordly, unphysical, a sort of mystical passion. She had the inscrutability of a Sphinx and lived in clean, prim poverty with her father who was a cutler from Sheffield. The boils and pussing eruptions that emerged on her skin in the last few months of her life seemed to me to be a lifetime's worth of silence and unspoken thoughts suddenly demanding to be heard all at once, and were so fierce as to kill her. Of course my daughter Ophelia was very upset at the time, but she was only a child and children heal quickly. She grew to love her stepmother and the love was mutual.

Which brings me on to her arrival. Right at the beginning. She was suffering from a broken heart: her husband had left her and she had been travelling alone through countless cities for too long. Her nerves were raw and she needed comfort. As both my daughters are called Ophelia, I will call her Ophelia 1 and my stepdaughter Ophelia 2. Being a scientist the equation $O^1 + O^2 = ?$ amuses me. There is something about the intricate symbols in science that is beautiful, almost miraculous.

I am in my laboratory. My wife is making a pair of shoes. My stepdaughter (O^2) is washing her long red-golden hair in the lake. The sound of hair hitting water, the air and light, the strange lullaby O^2 is singing . . .

> Sweet never weep
> For what cannot be
> For this has not been given
> If the merest dream
> Of love were true
> Then sweet we would be in heaven

and then my wife rinsing her hair for her, all made me feel very calm and happy. I am pouring liquids into tubes and can see everything from the glass doors of my lab. That was how I saw Ophelia[1] arrive! We all shouted 'Ophelia!' and ran to hug her. My wife told her she was making her a pair of shoes and had been trying to imagine her feet for days. Ophelia[1] tried to smile but we could tell she was sad. After a while I broached the subject of her husband.

'He's gone to Africa and South-East Asia,' she said.

O^2 was surprised. 'But he's always been so shy.'

'Perhaps he finds it easier to express himself in a tank.' Her nerves were in a terrible state. She kept slapping her body and complaining about the mosquitoes which, she said, were merciless. My wife and stepdaughter tiptoed through the shallow part of the lake and left us, father and daughter alone.

'Let's see some photos,' she said. She meant of her real mother, of our life together all those years ago. Reluctantly I fished them out from behind a stone, drenched and dripping as they were. She commented on how her mother looked like a statue waiting to be warmed into life, how long her neck was, the way her lips curled at the corners as if she was just about to speak. And then she cried and said she would like to have known her better, to see her now. I didn't know what to do. Then she pulled herself together and asked me how my work was going. I told her I had discovered what an atom looks like. When Columbus discovered land at least he knew what it was; he could identify it. Unlike land, until my recent discovery . . . years of exhausted searching in the dark . . . the atom could only be imagined in the mind's eye. She said she was pleased for me and proud that her father was such a clever man. I replied that I had no special gift, only passionate curiosity. And then my wife came in and said there was a man waiting for me. Apparently he had a piece of chocolate-brown metal to sell.

I left them together.

My wife said, 'See how rough my hands are. The wind and water chap them.' She took O^1's hand in her wide palm. 'I think all pain is to do with separation, in one form or another.' O[1] put the hand still clasped in her own on her belly. 'I'm pregnant,' she said blandly.

'Another pair of feet to make shoes for,' my good wife replied. You see, she understood, having brought up her own daughter alone. She was never sure who the father was, and in the end it didn't matter. Her daughter learnt how to read timetables at a very early age.

'He knew I had conceived before he went away.' O[1]'s voice was expressionless.

They were silent for a while. Breathing deeply in that position, hand in hand on my daughter's belly.

'Where have you been all this time?' my wife asked. It was not so much a question, as an invitation for O[1] to talk. It wouldn't have mattered if she hadn't replied. But she did.

'Wandering through pock marked cities. Deserted filthy streets. Sleeping in cheap hotels. I often spent days on end in pinball arcades listening to their silicone hearts shriek and shout through the leisure hours. I thought I'd write about it sometime. And then I saw, in every city and every port, lorry and ship loads of books and paintings being dumped into the sea, or in sewers, or on tips. I asked one lorry driver why. He said they were uneconomic. I knew I'd never write anything again. [She is talking very fast now.] I tried to get out of the cities. [I think her eyes are shut.]

'The countryside looked like a fodder factory. I met a farmer. He was using a picture as target practice. A painting of dark moist earth being ploughed, you could see the blades of the plough

48

in the brush strokes, and in the corner a small apple tree with its buds about to break open. I asked him if I could have that painting. I knew Ophelia would like it, but he was so busy shooting at it he didn't hear me. Later I heard that the artist, once very famous, died in a mental home quite near the farm, well when I say farm I mean a mass of cages and machines. The farmer drove to the home in his white Mercedes, found out which room had been the artist's, ripped the door off its hinges and sold it to an American. The same farmer that had used the truth of that artist's vision as target practice. So you see. I went away to make sense for myself.'

My wife listened to her, sometimes catching her eye, at other times looking away. It was obvious O[1] hadn't spoken to anyone for a long time. She seemed to have had her say and looked at her stepmother, a look so desperate – my wife told me this afterwards – that she had to search for words to answer it.

Ophelia[2] ran in carrying flowers. She'd just got back from the factory and her hands were orange from the dyes. She decorated her stepsister with the flowers . . .
'Fennel for welcome home
Camomile for long life
Violets for love . . . I only found two of those.'
O[1] kissed her and said two were better than nothing. And when a piece of cloth, woven that day in the factory, was draped around her shoulders, she said something about looking like this on her wedding-day, or was the cloth a shroud? I couldn't hear clearly because my visitor was saying goodbye to me.

'Sing us a song Ophelia.' My stepdaughter loves being sung to. And she did. With one hand on her belly while my wife measured her feet and O^2 plaited her hair.

> How should I your true-love know
> From another one?
> By his cockle-hat and staff
> And his sandal shoon
> He is dead and gone, lady.
> He is dead and gone.
> At his heels a green-grass turf
> At his head a stone . . .

She stopped suddenly. Staring straight ahead of her, breathing very quickly, her hand moving from belly to heart.

'What is it?' my wife asked.

'It's my mother,' Ophelia[1] said calmly.

The women all looked in the same direction. O^2 seemed near to tears. I wanted to protect her from my daughter's nervous hallucinations, but felt I would be intruding. 'She carries a string of burning flags, can you see her too?'

And my wife, horrifyingly, said 'Yes.'

'Stop it! Stop it!' O^2 was crying now.

And the last thing my deranged daughter, my poor, poor daughter whispered, was, 'The only thing I mourn for . . . is the loss of her hopes . . . whatever they might have been.'

As she said this, I was looking at atoms which have completely different physical properties, but nevertheless are chemically inseparable. I am grateful to science for allowing me to turn aside from the multitude of

50

things that clutter up the mind and direct it from the essential.

I am eating simple bread and cheese with my step-daughter O^2. She says she finds O^1 morbid. I ask her why and she doesn't answer. I don't think she feels qualified to talk about her, not having had the experience or the sorrow of O^1. She just says she saw a wedding at the local church yesterday, and the groom looked like O^1's husband. I suspect this young woman, who's never had a lover, has always been a little 'in love' with her stepsister's husband. Whenever he came to see us he always brought her a small present, something he knew she would like – and she always did. We enjoy each other's company, my stepdaughter and I. We don't have to talk much. I think she likes having a father, never having known her own. Strangely enough she is not at all curious about him. Sometimes I sing the song I made up in the lab for her.

O my darlings, O my darlings, O my darlings
ions mine
You are lost and gone for ever, when just
once you recombine

The song never fails to make her laugh. We're similar in that we both work hard and enjoy what we do. Like Galileo, I believe in the primal power of simplicity, and I have a feeling she does too. We have both been trained to simplify, we do not like complications. In a strange way, perhaps because she does not say much, she reminds me of my first wife. We finish our lunch and she goes back to the factory. I ruffle her hair affectionately – we are both still a bit shy about touching each other.

Dusk is my favourite time of day/night. It soothes

me. There are two reasons for this and they are both
to do with love. In my research I am sometimes reduced
to using parts of conflicting evidence, conflicting com-
plementary images. For example, there is no actual con-
flict in the conflicting appearance of the sky at noon
and the sky at night, it is much the same as electrons
behaving like waves and electrons behaving like par-
ticles, but don't let me bore you with this, let me get
on to the second reason. Dusk is the time of day/night
my wife and I sit together on a rock that has, over the
years accustomed itself to our varying contours. We
dangle our feet in the water and I run my fingers over
the love lines under her eyes and around her lips. I tell
her one day she'll turn into a piece of leather and she
laughs and splashes me with water. Her shoulders are as
broad as my first wife's shoulders were narrow. Slightly
freckled, they smell of thyme. I call her my heart and
run my hand up and down her warm supple back, glad
to be alive and nearest the one I love most. What entices
me about her (and this is going to sound contradictory
because I've already told you that I'm a simple man) is
that, even after all these years, I find her mysterious. I
think the most beautiful experience we can have is the
mysterious. It is the fundamental emotion that stands
at the cradle of true art and true science. She tells me
my daughter is pregnant. I say I don't understand her,
I feel helpless and guilty. After all a father should be
able to help his daughter when she needs it. To this she
replies, 'You can only do what you can do.' I like her
when she's practical like that (yes I know I must be
confusing you) and I fall in love with her all over again
when I hear her dark deep voice:

'I remember when I was a little older than her, also

pregnant, also looking for direction journeying to the shores of the Dead Sea. All I knew was that I wanted nothing to do with those who wield power. Oh it was a desolate landscape, parched, rimmed by mountains the colour of varicose veins. I could roll over and over in the water, smarting from the salt, I could even grip the arms of submerged trees as I swam. It was there I decided to make shoes. To learn the language of flesh and bone it seemed to me then, as it still does now, to be the most important language to learn. To think of shoes as a luxury is a corruption.'

While she is talking, I am thinking of all the shoes she has made me. The pair that are dearest are those she made when we first met. They are old now and look like clods of clay. She breaks my thoughts by asking about my work and whether I bought the metal from the man. I say yes, I did buy it, and am storing it in a plastic bag under a small rock; also that I intend to experiment with something called an 'A-Ray'. She asks me why I am doing these experiments. I say it makes me happy to find the cause of things. She thinks about this, and then says, her voice sharper than usual, too sharp for this time of day/night, 'I suppose knowledge that increases the quality of our lives is precious knowledge.' I tell her I love her. And touch her breasts. It is thrilling to think that by mere touch we can put most machinery to work, human and otherwise. I suspect our bodies are more complicated than any silicon chip but that, like the machine, there is an equation or formula that makes us operate, that enables us to complete a task, to serve our masters and mistresses. And ourselves. We make love and the gulls shriek above us.

It became obvious to us that O^1 was getting increasingly desperate as her belly swelled. She couldn't sleep at night and kept hallucinating her dead mother. She said the mosquitoes were cannibals and kept scratching her body until she was covered in sores and scabs. She talked to herself all the time, pondering over the so-called ghost of her mother. 'Why is this woman running circles round me? Is she a warning spirit? Does she need something to be done?'

I was very busy at this time, but one afternoon when she seemed more distraught than ever, I put my work to one side and went to talk to her. She snapped at me and said her 'neurosis didn't have a cube root' and if I couldn't comfort my own wife when she most needed help (she meant her real mother) why did I think I could comfort her? She became obsessed with the colour white. When she washed she sprinkled her body with salt, muttering something about catching leukaemia in the cities and that her white cells were eating up her red cells. She told my wife that when she was on holiday with her husband he swam in his shorts forgetting that his last traveller's cheque was in the pocket. She described how he nursed it to life; smoothing it, drying it in the sun, holding it to his chest 'as if it was a dying pigeon'.

Early one morning O^2 was making her way to the factory where she'd left some cloth to dry overnight and saw O^1 up to her waist in water, crying inconsolably, 'I fish and fish and fish and never catch anything that convinces me it's fighting for its life.'

Then my stepdaughter O^2 disappeared for three long days and nights. My wife went to look for her and discovered her sleeping under a willow tree. It was then we realised she was more upset and disturbed by O^1

than we thought (she always seems so calm) and couldn't face being near her. My wife brought her home, massaged her with mint oil, hugged and stroked her and told O¹ to pull herself together because she was upsetting her sister. O¹ replied curtly that there was a lot to get upset about considering the homespun cloth in the factory was so expensive to produce, only the rich could afford to buy it. This was a cruel thing to say because she knew it would hurt O² who is something of a Socialist. She inherits it from her mother who once hit me with the back of a shoe when I joked (it's unusual for me to joke) and said, 'I'm just a poor cowboy and don't want no government interference.' O¹ pulled the (white) feathers off a dead cormorant lying in the mud and then said wearily, 'Tell me about your factory Ophelia Two.' And she did:

'Tall poplars fringe the mill-pond.
Cottons bleach in the sun amongst the buttercups.
We make the dyes ourselves. The vats are chiselled from stone.
Outside the dyeing-room we often see trout leap in the air.
We work long hours and share the profit.
We each planted something we wanted to see grow and now we lunch in a garden full of lilac and marsh-marigolds.
We are often very tired.'

O¹ laughed a cruel laugh and said Utopias only exist in graveyards. My wife, who had been sitting quietly cutting leather unobserved, interrupted, 'She is saying what can be done with cloth and dye and gardens can be done with human minds and hands.' She was protecting her daughter of course. 'And what about his mind and hands?' I saw my daughter point in the direction of my laboratory. To my horror (my hands were trembling) I heard my wife say, 'What he doesn't understand is that our planet is as fragile as a sliver of apple peel.'

And I wanted to say to my wife/lover, and the man who interviewed me (before I died), 'Save Me From Myself. I don't know why I do what I do only that I have to see where it will lead me . . . this cataclysmic outpouring of energy. Facts throw light upon facts, I am consumed by the fire of facts . . . I know the Earth will be consumed by that same fire . . . the cold, calculating, empirical fire of facts. I burn here in my laboratory where I hatch out concepts not one of which I am certain will stand firm. Every notation is a blister on the skin of my fingers, and the skin of the Earth. Yes, I have, my beloved wife, stumbled on an equation of immense darkness but I want to tell you it was not through desire to hurt anyone, to cause pain, to annihilate a whole species. It was through an insatiable desire for harmony. Ophelia, I fear your murmurings. In wanting to protect you I also want to protect myself. We both know there is a kind of truth in madness. My wife, my heart, with you I burn too. Give me your hand, let me feel the valley between each finger, this map of human-beingness. It is then, in those small secret moments, I feel at peace, feel again a sense of wonder.'

But then I could never say that. Science is to do with precise knowledge. Everything is measured and put to the test. We wait for the results. It is not a cluster of tragic, inexplicable events like those that will occur throughout this story.

My daughter has taken to sleep-walking. Her belly is huge. She rejects food as if she wants to starve the life inside her. Her cheeks are pinched with hunger. She is terrified the child will look like her husband. Wading through the night water, slapping mosquitoes off her body, a stream of words come out of her mouth like the stream of salt she pours over herself:

> Your fingers have turned into bayonets
> Your heart into a bank
> Your penis into a skull . . .

My wife asked her whether she was rubbing salt into her wounds or whether she was trying to disinfect herself. She replied there was no point in asking questions anymore, questions did nothing for the economy, or something like that.

And then this obsession with white:

White Cherries
White Beans
White Bandages
White Canvas he used truth as target practice
White Mercedes he was only a peasant crawling under the car to see if it had left any dung the bribe from the government did not feed the land

And then the night that seemed to go on for ever:

> Oh my mother I see you again
> And again and again.
> I have a terrible feeling in my throat
> that you with your boils and sores
> Are the future
> come to haunt me.
> Your ears bandaged.

The damaged ear of The Twenty-First Century.
One eye smiling the other weeping
Oh I'm so sore here here here
[she touches her head, her heart, her belly]
I'm hungry. Feed me something
oh . . . oh . . . oh . . . oh . . .

We slept on. Pretending to sleep. My wife had her back to me. My hand on her breast, I could feel her heart beating. Later, much later, she told me my fingers stank of uranium. And through that long, terrible night, we could hear the sound of something being thrashed against a rock.

Ophelia[2] came home from work the next day, silent and tense. We thought she was just tired from all those hours of weaving, embroidering and dyeing. Then she told us O[1] had given birth. We were happy. She told us the baby had been drowned in a sack by her weeping mother. The sound of thrashing against the rock haunted us for a long time. My daughter seemed calmer. She began to eat a little.

My wife and O[1] are talking together. They don't know I can hear every word from the thin glass door of my laboratory. Everything seems to be a secret in my life these days. Eavesdropping conversations, pretending not to notice the tiny pair of shoes my wife must have made for our grandchild drifting out with the tide, and then, my secret conversations with the visitor who sells me metal.

O[1] is saying she wonders whether the Virgin Mary was also homeless and destitute. My wife asks her why she feels homeless. You see my wife is something of a migrant. I don't know what 'home' means to her. She has a few possessions which she carries around with

her, and her working tools. If you asked me to locate
her accent I wouldn't be able to – she has another name
and word for everything. When she handles money (and
she rarely does) she often confuses currencies. O^1 thinks
about the question (whenever she thinks hard her eyes
turn a deeper shade of blue), shrugs her shoulders and
says, 'When my father asked me what I wanted to be
when I grew up, I said I wanted to be an expatriate.
Now that I've grown up I try more and more not to
feel like one. This truly is a lonely century.'

My wife nods. Sometimes I think they're more like
sisters than mother and daughter. This thought disturbs
me – I find myself floundering as to which role I play
in the scheme of things. O^1 continues a little petulantly,
'Anyway, it's hard to feel passionate under a sky like
this.'

'Did you murder your child dispassionately?' My wife
looks at her feet.

'Yes.' They are silent for a bit. 'And I keep seeing
ghosts.'

My wife is still looking at her feet; she often does this
when she's at a loss for words. She looks up, 'Ghosts are
a speck of dust in the eye.' My daughter feels betrayed.

'But you saw her too!'

My wife answers, 'Perhaps.'

They both look so sad I nearly drop the substances
I'm holding.

'Say something nice to me,' O^1 pleads.

'No.'

'Are you cross with me?'

'No.'

'Do you think I should be more stoic than I am?'

'No.'

Having said 'no' three times my wife then says, 'We

have always been taught to look at the past and draw knowledge from it for the future. The truth of the future is in the present, you and me talking now, it would be foolish to pretend there's anything nice to say wouldn't it?' Sometimes I wish I didn't understand her.

A pure, sweet voice drifts over the lake. It is Ophelia[2] singing to herself. We all stop and listen.

> Tomorrow is Saint Valentine's day,
> All in the morning betime,
> And I a maid at your window
> To be your Valentine
>
> Then up he rose and donned his clothes,
> And dupped the chamber door;
> Let in a maid, that out a maid
> Never departed more . . .

O[1] scratches herself. 'My sister seems happy enough.'

My wife has her hand over her eyes. 'She's made a model of happiness for herself and clutches on to it and why shouldn't she?'

Again, that clear rippleless voice drifts over to us.

> By Gis and by Saint Charity
> Alack, and fie for shame
> Young men will do't if they come to't
> By cock they are to blame . . .

O[1] has made herself bleed. She says, 'She loved my husband.'

My wife says, 'Maybe. She treasures the gifts he gave her.'

'He loved her too.'

'Oh.'

'They often met.'

'Oh.'

'He used to lie to me.'

It is as if my wife cannot bear to listen – she interrupts and talks almost to herself:

'Perhaps she should see the cities? What do you think Ophelia One? But why should she? Too see "progress"? Capital? Learn to become a machine? She can't weave cloth in her medieval factory for ever. Why not? Progress has ceased to be on the side of reason. Let her have her ridiculous dreams, her marigolds, let them delight in yards of beautiful cloth they will later sell to the wives of business tycoons. Let them embroider sparrows and angels and cherries while the world eats itself out around them.'

They both wept. O^1 for her murdered child perhaps, I don't know why my wife wept. What I do know is that O^2, hidden in the shadows, heard every word of that conversation (another secret I have to keep) and every young bone in her body drained itself of any hope she had both for herself, and for the future. Her eyes were dry as theirs were wet. I was glad to lose myself in zinc sulphide which I note, emits a visible light when exposed to radioactive substances.

The sad afternoon arrived when my wife approached me. I was chopping wood. It is not a good task to be interrupted in because it is a private one. Finding the weak spot in the gnarled lumps, bending the knees, judging the right weight with which to wield the axe. Nevertheless we sat down together on the same rock we always sit on and I slipped my arm through hers. She said she could no longer live with me. I asked her if she no longer loved me. She said she did, but that she would have to kill that love. I didn't understand. And that's when she told me about my hands. How they smell of uranium. I say very little about my work to my wife, but she has a keen sense of smell. I replied (trying to keep my voice steady) that my work in the laboratory was quite different from my life with her and our daughters. She said a body carries all aspects of its life around with it all the time. I told her that I would never, could never, stop my research. I had started it and I would have to complete it, and anyway if I stopped there would always be someone to take over from where I left off. She said she could no longer be party to the violence of that research, especially since I was selling its secrets in exchange for substances that made my hands smell. So she knew.

I wrenched my arm away, she'd made me feel awkward about touching her. All I could say was, 'The fault is not with my atoms. It is with the people who use them.' I explained that I am a scientist, not a politician. I merely uncover possibilities, I don't make decisions. All I try to do is make physical sense. She stood up. We stopped talking. Frozen in our positions, I mean our geographical positions, me sitting she standing. I tried not to feel obsolete. Discarded before a fraction of my potential could be realised or appreciated. I was wearing the first pair of shoes she ever made for me. I always wear them to chop wood. My daughter Ophelia[1] broke the silence of our, so to speak, adopted attitudes. Her face as white as the obsession that haunted her. She told us Ophelia[2], my gentle happy stepdaughter, had drowned herself. Stupidly, all I could say was, 'How?'

'She decorated a willow tree with twists of barbed wire.

62

Made wreaths from nettles and stung her chest with them.
Put glass in her shoes.
Wound her hair round a slab of stone.
Waded into the water.
Said the trout were dead in the waters by the factory.
That workers were spitting blood over the cloth they wove.
That she heard a conversation that gave her no hope.
Sang something about there being more to life than just surviving it.
Ate the metal you bought from the man.
The waters she floats on throbs with uranium.'

And my wife cried, 'Oh we have failed her miserably! With our cynicism . . . our fatigue, our clever conversations . . . my beautiful red-haired daughter.'

She buried her head in her big hands and pulled at her cheeks, rocking from side to side.

'We will give her a splendid funeral,' I said. 'I will even sell my equipment to pay for it.' I think it was the shock that made me stupid. My daughter spat into the lake that had overheard my conversation of lovelessness with my wife, the lake that had swallowed up my grandchild and then my stepdaughter, that grey pool of mud and misery. My wife, still rocking, screamed, 'Perfume her corpse if you like, clean it, make it hygienic, blur everything with soft sympathy like you evade everything else, why don't you scream and shout man!!'

I went back into my laboratory and wept and wailed like a child. I wept for O^2, for my dead first wife, for my unhappy daughter O^1, for my beloved second wife who had pledged to kill her love for me, and for myself. At that moment, behind the glass doors of my feverish workplace, I felt as if I was on an island, without friends, allies or community.

They sat together. My wife and daughter. Staring straight ahead of them at the dirty gulls that had so often been our love chorus. My wife says at last, 'She hated clocks. She relied on the regular turning of the Earth. Myself, I always want to know the time.'

O[1] spoke very softly, 'I'm sorry.'

My wife goes on. I am for ever destined to watch and listen to her from a distance.

'She heard us talking and was upset, said to make a dream come true you have to make other people dream too, and then she said something strange. She said in the Middle Ages they would have built trains in the shape of dragons. I got irritated, told her to put both feet firmly on the ground.'

She is crying again. From here she looks like a large wounded beast.

'And now all I want to say to her, all I want to say to her is – It was a great idea Ophelia. To invent a time and place of your own. A time to live and a place to work. To have had an idea, and to have realised it, well there's an achievement. An idea needs recognition, encouragement, and help. Otherwise it drowns itself.'

My daughter's lips are blue. She says, 'I'm sorry.' My wife shuffled her feet.

'If what you mean is I feel more pain because she was my blood-daughter you're wrong. The pain would have been the same.'

She got up and walked a few steps, and then as if the effort were just too much, sat down again. She seemed to be be out of breath. My strong healthy wife.

'It's the air,' she said.

They both looked in my direction. I knew they could not see me, but all the same I felt dazzled. My wife sighs and turns to O[1].

'Go and talk to your father.'

That was how my daughter came to see me.

Usually I let no one into my workplace. It is private. But this time I did. I told her my wife was going to leave me. She nodded as if she already knew. She kissed me and said, 'Dad . . .', but at that moment she was interrupted because the journalist arrived, and embarrassed, I asked her to leave. Even while he was interviewing me (the man who sold me the metal has obviously been selling the equation I gave him in payment) I could see the women pointing. They both think they can see the ghost of my ex-wife. The one who died of the plague. I can only hear disjointed words, sighs, rustlings, and then distinctly, I heard my wife say, 'I have a feeling, at this moment, your father is pouring poison into his ears . . . because he can't find an equation for loss.'

The last thing I hear as the liquid runs into my ear drums (the journalist thinks this is an eccentricity and is asking me where I buy my clothes) is my wife, her arm linked through the arm of my daughter, saying, 'There she is. The Twenty-First Century. She looks more sad than angry.'

And my daughter, 'No. She's not angry or sad or run down. She's just poisoned.'

What I wanted to say before I died, particularly to my lovely wife, was that my role seems to have become more precarious, increasingly abstract, redundant. I am grateful to science and to love for making my life exciting and meaningful. Both can be destructive, in both we commit heresies, both are based on faith. Great science is not built on cold logic, nor is love, both require patience, intuition and sympathetic understanding. But none of this matters any more. If anything could grow in the poor soil around the lake I have polluted, and I had a last wish, I would choose rosemary. Rosemary for remembrance.

FLUSH

AS THEY STEPPED aboard *Oy Voy*, Iggy tried to explain to the pirate (who was after all interested in ships) that this was a ghost-ship and the invite had been slipped to her by capitalism's most up-and-coming Courtesan, a young man of melancholy disposition who wrapped himself in a garb of black designer cashmere and drank a lot of aniseed liqueur. The party tonight was financed by his employer, a balding American called Al Napalmski, and apparently held in honour of The Courtesan's diligent service to The Cause.

Deep in the bowels of the ship, small groups of pale and adorned people mingled exquisite hand gestures and perfumes, the dim light casting eerie shadows – a hand, a profile, a jaw angle, on to the wooden and slightly damp walls. Laden tables dripped with the over-flow of Al Napalmski's purse, and also his mistress Chintz, who reclined on the largest table of all idly squashing kiwi fruits against her very tanned and shapely thigh. Chintz was in fact a skilled physicist who had fallen on hard times due to a heretic theory, and now supported her young daughter, Medusa, with liasons such as these. On the table next to her, a whole roast pig stared out glassily at the rich pretty young things

OPHELIA AND THE GREAT IDEA

with very disciplined hairstyles to match their very disciplined bodies, who some time that evening would carve slices of succulent honeyrubbed flesh from her fat and once maternal belly. Chintz squashed the juiciest of all the kiwis against her own warm belly. She has just caught sight of Al Napalmski biting into a rabbit's paw dripping with garlic butter.

'My name's Sleeze. But people call me Sleeeeeeze,' pearldropped a Big-Bang businessman into the pirate's ear.

'Hi Sleeze.'

'Are you a real pirate?'

'Used to be. Wish *Oy Voy* had sailed the seas when I was in business.'

'Smart ship hey?' He inhaled from his asthma machine and then muttered something into his cordless phone.

'I'm a kind of pirate too, what made you give it up?'

'Love.' The pirate's eyes filled with moisture; it could have been sentiment or the ten hairy Big-Bang fingers stroking his nipples.

'Love?' The fingers probed more forcefully.

'Met my Iggy. A dove circled my ship seven times and I knew it was time to anchor my heart.'

At that the pirate started to cry, great gulpy sea-air sobs, and went off, nipples very bruised, in search of his beloved whom he found trying to escape from a one-eyed advertising bandit, a small book poking out of his bullet-proof shirt pocket entitled *A Hundred and One Ways to Get Rich, Get Laid, and Still Have Time to Destabilise Revolutions.*

'Have you ever considered . . .' he badbreathed, but had lost his audience who had fallen into each other's arms to recover from the blast of his inners.

68

All around them, glittering bodies manoeuvred proximity to each other with casual, supple gestures. The most distinctive were those that had cultivated a kind of high-energy ambience with which they gave expression to their full and fragile lives . . . 'I'm thinking of marketing a perfume called *Chernobyl*.' While draped over the marrons glacés, three media VIPs parading capricious and exotic swimwear compared tattoos and technological toys in streetwise accents. In the corner a group of black-suited architects with shaved heads agreed that the modern movement had been over-estimated and that 'laissez-faire stylism' is now what people will buy. Meanwhile Oscar and Natalie talk to the man from British Nuclear Fuel about marketing a strawberry-flavoured euthanasia pill. He points out that making it calorie free might boost sales. They nod their heads and swap phone numbers. In clandestine nooks and crannies, government officials eat cocaine on toast and plan cold wars over a glass of Guinness.

The globe strung to the ceiling transforms flesh to mercury as it silently and silkily makes its night breeze revolutions.

A Christian Scientist (self-confessed as this was the logo printed on his leather wedding-dress) points a sculpted black fingernail at Iggy who has placed two soothing oyster-shells over her eyes.

'Here.' He thrust a card into her hand.

'Can't read while I'm having oyster therapy.'

He snatched it back and read it to her extra loudly because everyone else was talking softly . . . 'Hadleigh Martin. Accountant. Bring your grit and lies to me, dash, I will turn them into pearls and truths.'

Click. Flash. The photographer stood on a chair capturing moments for the night, and what he caught at that moment was the amazing sight of The Courtesan, white as sin against the black of his cashmere, evaporate Hadleigh Martin. He simply melted into a wedding-gown puddle which began, slowly, to trickle like wayward veins in a body, down and across the laden, chattering, ship.

Click. Flash. The Courtesan tapped Iggy on her shoulder pad, his brutal eyes burning in the dim light.

'Glaaad you could come.' Those eyes seemed to suck her into some barren barbed-wire wasteland inside him. 'It makes me very happy to think that a shop-assistant can rub a limb with captains of industry at my parties.'

His attention was aroused by an eight-foot commercial giant with 'Virgin' tattooed across his naked left buttock. He excused himself and went to greet the Virgin with an erection.

'This place is full of demons,' husked the pirate, stuffing himself with rare roast-beef.

A heavenly breeze suddenly caressed the worldwounded cheeks of all aboard. It seemed to be coming from Chintz who was notating a few inky equations on her gently muscled arm.

'That was no demon. More like an angel,' growled back the Twentieth-Century Hermit, who smelt very raw in a fringed buckskin jacket. 'Know what these fringes for?'

'What's that sister?'

'Allows the rain to run off, an' breaks up my outline so wild beasts can't get me easy.' Her lonely eyes settled on Chintz's perfect breasts and, yes, Chintz smiled a wild clover smile back and even blushed slightly.

'Many wild beasts in the city?'

'Naw. I live beside the River of No Return.'

'Aha.' The pirate offered her a crisp.

'Usually eat bear crackling.' Chintz was laughing. The Hermit wanted to tell her that bear crackling was bliss when dipped into a little goat's cheese, but then she was not used to talking to people.

'I like you sister,' Pirate husked a little more gently than before. He pointed to Chintz. 'So does she.' Encouraged, the Hermit dug her hands into her buckskin pockets and took out a piece of bark. 'Got a pen?' Pirate explained he didn't believe in them. At last, the Hermit opened her mouth wide, wrenched out one of her teeth and scratched a map into the bark.

'Here. Come visit me some time. I'll bake ya a holy fish.'

Pirate studied the map for sometime. 'I'll bring my ma, usually take her out on Sundays,' and then he walked over to Chintz and gave the map to her. Chintz smiled a sleepy smile which made the Hermit's brown body shake all over. Only yesterday she had hunted wild bear with steady hand and heart, she cursed her body for letting her down at such a profound moment. How was she to know that Chintz, now being fondled by Al Napalmski, was making secret plans to take her daughter on a love journey to the River of No Return?

'Iggzzzzzzzzzzzzzz.'

A woman with dazzling red hair pushed her way through a crowd of stockbroker poets in midnight blue suits and drip-dry J. F. Kennedy shirts. She appeared to be buzzing. Iggy, who was soaking her swollen shop-floor feet in a bowl of warm beer (the *Oy Voy* chef, a Mexican magician, had prepared the remedy for her saying it was the best thing to do when feet complained about the servile nature of their lives), saw to her surprise that the woman buzzing towards her was an old friend who used to work on the tills with her, Germaine.

Germ for short on account of all the diseases she thought she had after buying a medical encyclopaedia. How she had cursed that salesman! It is rumoured that his lungs collapsed soon after.

'I'm all lack-lustre Igzzzz,' Germ draped herself over Iggy and wept.

'I don't know what there is to hope for any more.'

A group of millionaire teenage bankers in combat jackets and Gucci jewellery playing Trivial Pursuit in the corner begin to sing patriotic songs in perfect harmony. Al Napalmski taps his white canvas shoes and bites into another rabbit's paw, spitting the bones delicately into a silver bowl on his lap. The Head of Police who has lined up a row of boiled goose eggs smashes them with his truncheon, much applauded by the government officials. As he smashes the seventh egg, he tells them he is a prophet and that his truncheon is merely God's right hand.

'Remember Cindy?' sobbed Germ.

'The woman who grew cacti in her husband's shoes?'

'Yeah. She left a little message in a perfume bottle under her pillow, something about dying unarmed in that madhouse he put her in. I don't know where the doctors buried her.'

Iggy's tears spilt shamelessly onto the bare boards of *Oy Voy* as had many tragedies, love juices and evaporated bodies before her.

'They're pecking our spirits bare as bone Iggzzzz.'

Germ wailed so loudly that one of the stockbroker poets, inspired, began to write an ode for the *Surrey Post* on his shirt cuff. But Iggy knew better because at that moment she saw Chintz wink at Germ, her green dagger eyes reflected in the puddle of tears by her feet. And what's more, the little suitcase Germ held tightly in her hand (it had a red cross on it) was indisputably, perhaps irrevocably, buzzing.

But something even more extraordinary is happening deep in the bowels of *Oy Voy*. Two dwarfs in leopard-skin booties dance across the tables swinging heavy gold censers. The ghostly sound of an organ playing rocks the boat from left to right. Soon everyone is choking. Rumour has it that the censer contains frankincense and tear-gas. It is through this swirling mist of both chemical and heavenly fragrance, and dizzy-making organesque, that Al Napalmski wearing a FEED THE WORLD tee-shirt, followed by The Courtesan carrying a blue Perspex heart on a satin cushion, slowly, breath-takingly, emerges. As The Courtesan kneels in front of the heart, his very white fingers are clasped in monetar-ist prayer. The parasites living in the laughter of those aboard *Oy Voy* fly out and dance a merry dance on the head of the roasted pig. Al Napalmski continues: 'I'm not a man to beat about the bush only thing I ever beat about was my ex-wife an' all my dorters so I'll say wot I have to say an' say it strait. Yung tycoons must be snapped up when innicent an' nurtured. They gotta grow up in the right enviromint an' giv'n the right thorts to think. In other words we gotta grow 'em a human nature, an' I grew my Courtesan's in the company greenhouse.'

The Courtesan brushes a disturbance from his cheek. At that same moment, a seagull swooping over the water that hosts *Oy Voy* is impaled on her radio mast. As its blood drips into the sea, the bleached lips of The Courtesan begin to fill with colour.

The excitement has made Al Napalmski breathe more heavily so that the map of the world on his belly becomes whole continents, heaving, rippling, falling and rising . . . 'Wot I like 'bout this boy is he ain't over perceptive an' under productive like a lotta brash bean hash these days. He ain't gotta histerical perspektive of things an' his heart ain't his favourite organ.'

Bzzzzzzzzzz. Germ's pearly fingers silently open the little Red Cross suitcase. A million bees make honey inside it. 'I firmly believe that these qualities, his savage individualism, heroism, miserabilism, torturism . . . his love of liberty, pertrolium barbarian burgers an' gherkins . . . hell ladies an' gents I'm drunk . . . wot I'm trying to say, yeah, he don't like natural environments an' he likes the thort (we gave it to him in the lab) of tampering wit the stars 'cos men of curiosity an' initiative always desire to conker the unknown. My boy ain't just a bag o' brains he got a cock, hell wot I'm trying to say in my own sweet way is that I need an heir. I got no sons an' my dorters hate me. Whatdayasay son?' Chintz slides her hand into a crystal bowl full of trifle. She takes out a small shiny revolver covered in cream and cherries. The Courtesan scratches an itch on the left side of his nose. At that moment a fish which has been sleeping beside a rock explodes into a mass of bubbles and suds.

'Whatdayasay son?'

'I am honoured Sir, and can only hope my obvious youth and inexperience will dissolve like a Disprin as I acquire a working knowledge of state corruption and thus achieve excess for all who deserve it least.'

As people whoop, pop corks and put their tongues in unspeakable orifices, Iggy removes her shoulder pads which are soaked in ether. She nods at the Hermit who takes out a little wooden bow and arrow from under her buckskin jacket. Al Napalmski picks at the bits of sinew and gristle between his front two teeth. He staggers a bit so that his bodyguards have to lunge forward to hold him up. He takes a deep rancid breath. 'Ladies an' Gentlemen . . . I formally hand over my heart to this young man in front of all yous witnesses . . . all my white papers, pink papers an' yella papers . . . all my sekrets, all my kash.'

Click. Flash. The Courtesan now on his feet, hugs the blue Perspex heart to his own beating heart. They have become one heart.

It is possible that at any moment now, bees, bullets, ether and little poisoned arrows will become the instruments of chaos, truth, revolution, revenge. It is also possible that at this moment the pirate is on the deck, sleeves rolled up, preparing *Oy Voy* for a voyage of his own.

The moon is full and bloody. But the photographer isn't paid to notice the moon. He is a busy man.

HERESIES

I

A MAN WALKED out into the Dutch dawn with sixteen candles burning on the rim of his hat. He took out his easel and began to mix colours. He painted the light and the candles burnt with him.

An expert on art appointed by the state walked the polished corridors of a gallery selecting paintings to serve the state. He stopped abruptly in front of this painting and demanded the artist be interrogated by the Chief of Police. The Chief of Police typed out a report of this interrogation in which the artist is claimed to have said: 'I allowed light to change the perceived notion of things.' The artist was sent to a mental asylum where he remained for three years and on his release shot himself in a field throbbing with sunflowers.

Years later another man wrote of this same artist: 'He was a man suicided by society.' The man wrote this from a mental asylum where he remained on and off for sixteen years. During his time there he wrote plays for the theatre in which he demanded 'light be used to evoke delirious emotions', and countless essays which were only published after his death when he became a cult martyr. He also graffitied every possible wall in the asylum with things like, *Trying to define us is like trying to bite your own teeth . . . Although your information is incorrect I do not vouch for it . . . A banker will only lend you money if you can prove you don't need it.* A cleaning woman was sent at regular intervals to dissolve the graffiti with a specially prepared solution.

Fifty years later a young woman takes her washing to a Turkish launderette in a broken part of East London. The walls are mosaiced with hundreds of tiny coloured stones, woven here and there with jagged pieces of shimmering mirror. Outside the streets are wet, scattered with litter and small shops are open for Sunday trading. The door opens and an ornate Turkish Tramp King carrying a small basket and battered radio shuffles in and sits down. A golden diamanté crown sits on his coarse grey hair and small jewels entwine his beard. They are shaped like eyes. His robes are exotic and filthy, layers and layers of chiffon, cotton, wool and satin, various lengths and textures. Outside, the chip shop is opening its doors and a queue of pale skinned, round shouldered people clutching purses and smoking cigarettes clamber to get out of the rain. The Turkish Tramp King seems to enjoy the rhythm of the washing machines, rocking to and fro, sometimes scratching, humming a little, relaxed and completely at home. Delicately, he cups his head into his hands, and still upright, falls into a light, contented sleep. The laundry-woman walks in with a bag of chips in her hand, sees him, shouts, 'filthy dog', takes off her slipper and starts to beat him. He shouts at her, gesticulating wildly with his hands, the rings on his fingers glittering in the artificial light. She drags him to the door and throws his eighty-year-old body out into the street. She is the daughter of the cleaning lady who once dissolved all the graffiti in the asylum.

The psychiatrist in the asylum the Turkish Tramp King is sent to writes this report (a translator was present) of their first conversation:

2 pm on very cold Sunday afternoon I am tired so walk to palace my oldest son build for me for siesta. I delouse myself and find happiness in sleep. I am awoken by stranger shouting at me and beating me in face with shoe. She push me into street and break my radio.

The psychiatrist is the grandson of the doctor who strapped electrodes on to the red head of the artist, and he in turn will strap electrodes on to the grey head of the Turkish Tramp King.

II

Nato planes fly at regular intervals overhead. The sky muddy as the peat soil below. Sparse scattered grass. Bleak flat fields. Filthy goats scavenge for shrubs. A long dull view. In the distance borstal boys build a seawall that does not need to be built; they are not unaware of this fact. Each has an orange number tattooed on the back of his donkey jacket. Further on, where the land is ploughed, small frozen waves of soil. North sea winds. The planet stripped to its lowest common denominator. Sky and Earth.

'Are you contracepted?'

'Yes.'

The landscape a physical expression of all that is

bleak and stripped inside. At this moment it is possible to imagine the ghosts of one hundred million of our species slaughtered in the last sixty years, rising from the dark earth in terrible accusing silence.

'I suppose I should have asked you that before.'

'Yes. I suppose you should have.'

They are lying in an old rowing-boat called 'Noble Savage' parked on a desolate beach. Sea gulls swoop and shriek above them, sometimes disappearing into the grey sea.

'My great-grandfather,' he says, doing up his flies, 'was a God-intoxicated man . . . ein Gottbetrunkener.' He runs his fingers lightly down her arm. She lies there and wonders whether she loves or hates him. Her silence disturbs him, as does the lonely thrashing of the sea and the gulls searching for food. He is the great-grandson of the artist who placed candles on the rim of his hat to achieve a light he felt to be true and she is the granddaughter of the writer who graffitied the asylum. After a while he asks how the plot is developing in the play she is currently writing for a theatre in London.

'I'm not interested in plot.'

'How many characters will there, be?'

'I'm not interested in characters.'

He is not sure how serious she is. 'Narrative?'

'I'm not interested in narrative.'

He picks at a splinter in his finger, 'Are you cross with me?'

She shuts her eyes:

Plato and Aristotle lie in a shady bower somewhere in Athens, buggering each other. Plato takes out a small jar of olive oil. Aristotle flinches, 'I want you to fuck me not fry me.' Plato frowns as he applies

80

the oil ... 'I see I will have to sodomise your poetic inclinations Aristotle. Your emotions are disorganised and you only understand the world in an illusory way' ... he thrust more brutally than usual. Aristotle is in considerable pain ... 'Plato ... to deprive a man of his emotional equipment is to make him a useless ethical cipher ... Zeus! ... what are you doing to me! without even the potential for goodness.' Plato is sweating and about to have an orgasm ... 'The emoti ... emo ... emotions aroused in po ... poet ... ry ... are those of infection ... and ... can ... can ...

only lead to eeeeeeeeeeeexcess!' He stifles his cry and collapses, flushed and breathless. Aristotle, who is neither flushed nor breathless, composes a little ditty:

> Plato, You declare war
> On emotion and unreason –
> To see it any other way
> You consider treason.
> In this respect you are not
> So different from Nato.

Aristotle resolves to devote his life to poetics and start up a school for young philosophic Greek men. They will learn plot construction, character, unity of action and narrative. To see it any other way will be considered treason.

She opens her eyes to discover the gulls have been replaced by a Nato plane hovering above their boat.

He is sitting in the audience watching the first night

of her play. For some reason he feels vulnerable and irritated; the intense atmosphere of the theatre, burning lights, rose-water, talc, the pile of black roses heaped on the stage, the hypnotic beating of the drums, the ornate head-dresses of the drummers which appear to be paper structures of the Chamber of Commerce, leave him fumbling for words to express what it is that irritates him. He is aware that some kind of magic is being worked on him and resents this; he is aware that the magic is 'female' in some way; he is thinking the stage should be purged of everything magical if it is to be of critical importance to the working-class. He is toying with the idea she might be idealogically unsound. Something is on fire: the Chambers of Commerce, previously blessed by the priest, are now being burnt. The drumming has stopped; his argument is formulated: impulse and imagination are corrupt luxuries of the bourgeoisie. One of the actors walks on with a life-sized puppet which he starts to undress and as the puppet is stripped naked it becomes clear the actor is a jailor. The doll has a nervous system drawn outside its body. Three more jailers/actors enter. The first jailer is now giving a lecture using the life-sized puppet to demonstrate the social system of the body. He leans back in his chair irritated again and notices the critic sitting in front of him who has been scribbling in a bored ostentatious way, and now very noisily stands up and makes his way out of the theatre. Their eyes meet fleetingly.

Social system of the body? He is currently writing a book on 'The Social System' and has formed a collective of specialists to research the subject. Something comes to mind, a dinner party to which he'd invited some of these researchers. She was grating carrots for the salad when they asked her about her work. She said it seemed at least as advanced or radical to attempt a more social art as not to. While she was talking she had by mistake grated her knuckles and the carrots were covered in blood. He had wondered at the time why attempting a more social art was even debatable.

An elderly actor in a timeless suit places his fingers arthritically on the yellowed keys of a Bechstein piano and begins to play a distorted version of *The Red Flag*. This character has appeared before and is known as 'The Heretic'. He begins to speak in a broken East European accent: 'My friends in the party used to say to me, Jacob, you play the piano like you talk politics, you ramble in and out of sense. We don't always understand your argument at the time but afterwards, well. So they listened to me, in their own way. Come the Twentieth Congress and Stalin's activities are out in the open, they said now is the time, Jacob, to come to the aid of the party. You must make sense in the light of what has happened, the people's spirit must be raised, their faith renewed, you can serve them. Give up this obscure nonsense you are composing . . . the people will not listen . . . it tells them nothing of their lives. And I replied, the people must then be taught to listen. I am myself a person.'

He takes a perfect, pulpy, honey-coloured pear resting on the musty surface of the piano and throws it up to the ceiling.

'Science after all, is only relative.' The pear does not fall down again. 'What purpose does realism serve? I asked – are images of starving children, beaten workers, brutal factory owners, realistic? Myself I think they are absurd. Music, like revolution must be a celebration of all the senses, a celebration of what human beings are capable of making. So. What is to be done? First, we must locate the vision . . . the imagination that helps us to see. If capitalism teaches us to see we must then re-learn how to look. If capitalism teaches us how to hear we must then re-learn how to listen.'

A profusion of blossom litters the city, for the entire spring. Ice-cream vans do their rounds earlier than usual, buds sprout even in the most desolate of soil, city cats frolic in the early sunshine. Oxfam stops sending aid to the third world and concentrates on the immense poverty sprawling over England like white film over a blind eye. An expert on art appointed by the state to fund art that serves the state, decides to put an end to all arts subsidies, with the exception of ballet, opera, a state orchestra, a state theatre and one literary magazine that will continue to pretend England is an old, cultured, gentleman instead of a small businessman frightened of books and theatres and ideas.

III

The sun in Haiti is blistering his red complexion. He puts his hand over his eyes and resolves to visit the barber in the afternoon. An elderly black woman shuffles out of the whitewashed house carrying a tray of iced lemonade and a hat. She clicks her tongue when she sees his burnt face and neck: 'Tonton you must protect yourself from the heat. It is not good for a European to face the sun bareheaded.' She pours out the lemonade and he puts the hat idly on his head.

'Thank you Matine.' He gulps the iced drink gratefully and she pours him out some more using her other hand to scatter flies.

'No calls for me today?'

84

'I have been shopping for your dinner all day Tonton . . . if I am busy as yesterday with your calls I will have faiblesse.' She has learnt good English over the years as a servant to European visitors, but every now and again breaks into her native creole. 'You are very famous man.' She laughs. 'Elite.' He is a famous man. His first book was an international success and on most university book lists, his second equally successful but more specialised, and now he has been commissioned to write a third entitled *The Social Implications of Voodoo in Haiti*. As universities have either had their funding halved or closed down in England, this might not sell as well as the others. However, the fact that he is the great-grandson of the famous artist has been instrumental in helping to sell the books; it is mentioned on every cover in every language and even been the subject for a slim paperback comparing them. What he has inherited is admirable self-discipline, although he has used this to excavate scientific and rational data for academic study, rather than find form for emotional and social disorder as his great-grand-father did. He also has the added distinction of a lobe-less ear which is said to have been removed in a fight he had many years ago with a lover in England. Apparently he told her mayonnaise was ideologically unsound.

'Tonton, will you eat rice tonight?'

'Matine I will eat whatever you cook for me.'

She shuffles back into the house to wash the rice.

He looks up at the cloudless sky and is dazzled by the light.

After she came out of the asylum for mutilating her lover's ear, a kind of novelty attached itself to her name thus ensuring a large audience for anything she chose to do. She was silent, saw nobody and wrote nothing.

Her supporters soon dwindled, taking refuge in a form of extreme esotericism appreciated by a handful of esoteric people. Later on, most of them took financial bribes and filled their large houses with priceless paintings and burglar alarms.

Two winters later when the few remaining trees in her neighbourhood were chopped down by the local council, she created a 'happening' in the Turkish launderette. Local mothers, fathers, grandparents and children participated. The chef from 'The Sultan's Kitchen' played the Turkish Tramp King, the Greek mama from the grocery store decided to stop hating the Turks for a day and played the Turkish Tramp Queen – they were married by children from the estate with much sprinkling of multicoloured washing-powder. The librarian composed the music with the doner kebab man – a stormy partnership due to grease on the score and a conflicting sense of rhythm, a Chilean car worker cracked toy junta soldiers between her teeth, a woman just released from Holloway Prison for breaching the peace graffitied a broken clothes wringer with: 'The English for London is Washington', and three Jamaican girls limbo danced into the tumble driers. The woman from the chip shop played the laundry-woman who beat the Turkish Tramp King with her shoe. He told her how he'd been stripped of his homeland and she told him how she'd been evicted with her young daughter by the bailiffs for not being able to pay the rent. Together they come to the conclusion they share a mutual homelessness and have been exiled from wealth they helped to create in the first place. The laundry-woman offers the newly-weds a free wash in the machines to celebrate, and the Greek mama forgets she is playing the Turkish Tramp Queen for a minute to tell the laundry-woman she always does her washing by hand because she never trusts machines. The chorus sings its last song happily and badly and everyone gets ready for a procession down the road to 'The Sultan's Kitchen'. Here, a drunken, messy, abundant and glorious feast is being prepared by dispossessed people, for dispossessed people. They will toast each other and celebrate the magic that is theirs, saving their scraps for the boss-eyed cat whose stomach is swollen with kittens.

PASSION

THE VERY WHITE room contains three things at this moment; on the walls, a series of photographs showing Winston Churchill, first as a young baby in a white cotton frock, then as a smooth-cheeked adolescent, then as a young man in a flying hat (tweed), and lastly as a balding fat man. Part of this composition includes a wooden bow tie painted blue, and next to it a long thick cigar in an aluminium container entitled 'Romeo Y Julieta'. A radio standing on the polished cabinet lets out a BBC voice. Its context is not clear:

> I felt there was a grandeur about it all.
> Those wounded men were calm and at peace
> with everything, so that pain seemed a
> small thing with them. I felt there was
> a spiritual ascendancy over everything.

A man, probably in his mid-thirties, sits on an upturned orange box. Around him are a few sheets of blank paper. Every now and again he takes a blue silk handkerchief out of his pocket and wipes his nose. It is winter and there is a hint of snow in the pattern of the clouds; the man has pulled two white blinds over the windows of the room. With his right hand he draws vertical lines on a piece of paper, his spine very straight, while the fingers of his left hand gather towards the centre of his palm and then unfold again. The gesture could be one of impatience, while the almond contours of his fingernails suggest time and care. There is a knock on the door.

His lover is tall and wrapped in a camel wool coat. She wears very flat brown leather shoes and carries a parcel in her arms. They kiss against the very white walls, his hand pressed lightly on the small of her back. She kisses first the crevice of his neck which is slightly scented, then the tip of his ear, and finally the thin lines of his lips. He touches her breast through the deep pink chiffon of her blouse. She kisses his fingers, light moist kisses. When they finally reach her nipple it is her own warm spit she feels. He pours them both a whisky and they sit by the fire. She watches him unwrap the parcel in four swift movements. Inside the silver wrapping-paper sits a stricken-looking stuffed fox, glazed eyed and glossy haired. She tells him it belonged to her grandfather and she would like him to have it. They look at the fox from different angles, at a distance, close up, from left to right, until all possibilities exhausted, he puts it on the cabinet below the pictures of Winston Churchill. She is looking through the papers he has been drawing on, now and then taking sips from the whisky in her glass which is emerald and has a very long, slim stem. He stands next to her and explains that he is designing a building for a town centre. The nature of this building is that it must be constructed out of the cheapest materials available, be functional and unclut-tered in shape. He, however, plans to contrast the clean vertical lines of the building by placing a solitary Corin-

PASSION

thian pillar next to it. He does not know whether this
structure will sell.

The whisky is nearly finished. The man and his lover
sit side by side. Disentangling her arm from around his
neck, she reaches over and makes a paper aeroplane
out of one of the blank sheets. She makes a whirring
noise in her throat and flies it into his groin. He slides
his hands between her legs, finds another sheet of paper
and makes a second aeroplane. It lands between her
breasts. While he sucks her nipple she makes more
aeroplanes. They call them names like 'Phantom', 'Whirl-
wind', 'Fairy Fox', 'Mama'. She says her aeroplane
has a Rolls Royce engine. He says his aeroplane is about
to crash.

It is predicted that snow is going to fall. It is very
cold. The man is walking down a busy street, hands
thrust deep into his pockets where he has placed a
Japanese hand warmer. Its charcoals are reputed to
burn for twelve hours. The wall he passes is graffitied
with the words: 'Workers of the World Untie'. He walks
into a café on the Finchley Road and orders an apple
juice. In the last three months he has developed a kidney
complaint and has been told by the doctor to give up
alcohol for a while; he has also found that his diet has
changed to one of vegetables rather than meat. Around
him, sitting at various tables, are an assortment of
Jewish immigrants. To his right sits a woman in her
early sixties, one arm slumped over the shoulder of her
companion. She has sagging breasts and lazily holds a
cigarette between fingernails painted a deep orange. The
ash is about to fall. Straight ahead of him an elderly
lady slowly drinks soup; she has not taken off her fur
hat and her cheek bones suggest a history of sorts. He
remembers these women from his childhood days in

91

Swiss Cottage; at the time his father had moved a lover into their home. His mother had done her washing for her, sometimes peering at the labels of various garments, and then, feeling observed, returning to the task in hand.

He is waiting for a woman friend. He has not seen her for a year. At the back of his wardrobe hang a few garments which belong to her; they have a distinct fragrance he has not been able to remove. When she arrives he notices a small round pearl in her ear, and remembers that in ancient mythology the pearl was a symbol of tears. She wears zebra-skin shoes and carries three plastic bags which appear to be full of clothes, letters, books, and what look like two saplings in small pots, covered with a protective layer of cellophane. A lilac wax rose-bud, a kind of hair-grip pinning up her dark hair, trembles slightly. Her lips and hands twitch from time to time and this mildly disturbs him. She has to wait for the right moment before she can hold the continental coffee to her lips which have gone slightly purple from the cold. He makes a private note to give her the Japanese hand warmer as a gift, and asks if she has been getting enough sleep recently. She says she thinks her mattress is full of bed bugs and this gives her bad dreams. She holds the handle of one of her plastic bags as she speaks:

I dreamt I was walking through an industrial beach in Spain. There were sewage pipes pumping into the sea and two boys sitting on white stone boulders, fishing. One of them asked me for a cigarette. As I fumbled for my bag the two heavy bracelets on my arms clinked, and the boy grabbed the cigarette, all the time looking at the silver on my wrists. My mother had bought me these bracelets so that

I could sell them if I ever got into trouble and needed money urgently. The beach was surrounded by slums, washing hanging out, people sitting on doorsteps, the walls sprayed with countless hammers and sickles. I remember thinking Franco must have had rich pickings from this area. Part of the beach was very flat and had two disused railway lines running across the grey shingle. An aeroplane circled low over the area. A man came up to me with some sort of machine in his hand and ordered me to walk past him three times so he could see what direction the needle of the machine would fall in. I did so; he shouted to the two boys sitting on the rocks and they immediately grabbed me by the arms. The machine was a Jewometer specially designed to round up Jews in the area. At one point you walked past us, two technicians at either side of you, rolled up plans under your arm. The man with the Jewometer machine congratulated you. Our eyes – yours and mine – met for a moment and then you looked away. I was told to take my shoes and socks off so that my feet could be examined.

She now takes the cup of continental coffee and drinks from it. He is aware that the people around them have been listening. The ash has fallen from the orange fingernails. The woman in the fur hat is slowly cutting through the white meat of a veal schnitzel. The knife scrapes the plate. Someone coughs and fumbles for a tissue. He takes her hand. It is rougher than it was a year ago. She smiles at him and says she has become a farmer. He tells her he has just sold a design for a building in a town centre. She congratulates him. He is wearing a wooden bow tie painted blue. She is wearing a chipped seashell necklace. They are trying to retain the moment. Sometimes they catch a look in the other's eye which suggests other moments. When this happens they look away.

They catch a bus together. She has eighteen stops to go, he has five. He makes a present of the Japanese hand warmer; together they discover the charcoal is still smouldering. He tells her he has missed her in the time they have been apart. She plays with her hair, talks about the trees on her farm, the balmy light, the bronchial owls, the trout leaping out of the river, how to avoid being chased by a bull by walking in zigzags, shuts her eyes, opens them, fingers her shell necklace, talks about bees, moths, snails, wipes her eyes, talks about spiders, mosquitoes, worms, tide timetables, yeast, axe handles, and smiles at a baby girl sitting near them. She has two plastic bags on her lap, one by her feet, and thirteen stops to go. They arrange to see a film in the near future.

From behind the walls of the very white room drifts the sound of a piano playing a sad barbed waltz. Solitary and limpid, it is the sound of discord. The man now wears cream woollen knickerbockers and stands by his drawing-board. The wire bin in the corner is full of crumpled paper aeroplanes and a wreath of pencil sharpenings. As he draws, very delicately and precisely, he listens to the waltz coming in from behind the walls and tries to solve the riddle of its components, now and then looking at the ordered lines on his paper with satisfaction. Eventually he takes this sheet of paper and knocks on the very chipped paintwork of a door next to his very white room. The waltz stops, continues, stops again, as if pausing to resolve the melody that has been interrupted, until finally the door is opened by a middle-aged, grey-hatted gentleman, who ushers the intruder inside and points to a red velvet chair for him to sit on.

The room is dark and smells of candle wax, the walls covered with various posters of concerts, theatre events, Indian Gods, Lenin, a fat smiling Buddha, a plaster car inscribed 'Van Gough' and scrawled underneath this 'Me', while faded almost beyond recognition the inside of a record sleeve pinned to the wall and about to drop, graffitied with 'I am fundamentally opposed to Germanic "absolute" music'.

The gentleman makes tea from a gas ring in the corner of the dark room, tapping the teapot with a small silver spoon as if moving in time with some invisible rhythm still alive in his body. The man in the cream, woollen knickerbockers lights a thick cigar, leaning his very blond head against the dark red of the velvet settee. He says he made good money from a bank he designed for a town centre, that his particular idiosyncrasy, namely the Corinthian pillar, had been noted and lauded; now he had been commissioned to design a swimming-pool for two Arab princes. He blows out two blue circles of smoke and stretches out his legs. The middle-aged gentleman pours the tea, hands a cup to the intruder, and says, eyes to the floor: 'We will take the hammer to your Corinthian pillars.' The white knickerbocker man laughs. He rolls his head and mouths the word 'puritan', staring at a photograph of a small dark woman with slanting eyes and a faint moustache on her upper lip. She is smiling shyly out of a tortoise-shell frame. He repeats himself: 'Puritan. I will make waves where there are none. And achieve perfect beauty, strength, health, harmony, in the making of this pool.

Perhaps I will use light; any mood can be evoked by trick perspective.'

The middle-aged gentleman stirs his tea. And continues to do so. His wrist is as relaxed and steady as his voice: 'Creativity is directly related to the physical and moral states of its makers.' He takes his cup to the piano and begins to play the waltz as before. The white knickerbockers shift. 'Is that your wife?' he points to the photograph. 'Yes.' The waltz stops abruptly. 'Why do you ask?' 'I have always had an affinity with women from the Ukraine and Lithuania.' The middle-aged gentleman places his hands on the yellowed keys, his voice comes out peculiarly shrill: 'My wife must have made a very pretty lampshade.' He continues to play and does not stop until he hears the intruder tiptoe out, shut the door, and walk a good length of the communal corridor.

A woman swathed in bandages sits in a wheel-chair in the cell of a prison in Ireland. She is listening to a tape through plastic earphones. Behind her, a young English prison wardress has her finger on the button controlling the tape. Her hair is scraped into an immaculate bun and when she claps her hands, making 'Hup Hup' noises, the woman gets out of her wheel-chair and starts to shout in Gaelic. The film has another hour to run and its end is not predictable.

The woman with the pearl in her ear lies on her stomach, naked, across the bed. The man who owns the white knickerbockers and navy-blue raw silk jacket draped over the chair sits on her bottom massaging her back. He is wearing a vest. She has put her long-stemmed glass of wine next to the sturdy plant with the damp pink bandage wrapped around its stem: every now and again she reaches for the glass and takes a tiny lingering sip of the rich wine inside it. He pours some oil on to her spine and says: 'Explanation is not always necessary.' She lies beneath him and says nothing. He continues and the tone of his voice changes a little. 'You gave me a taste for passion.' The pressure of his hands increases a little. She is thinking about change, he is kneading her lumbar as she recalls how certain traits continue – although they appear transformed as something else – how a tribe called the Nuba performed their Nazi rituals in the desert. She tries to breathe quietly. His fingers are now on her neck, stroking gently, he presses a little harder. The balls of his thumbs go white. Her muscles suddenly spasm; she flings out her arm which catches the long-stemmed glass full of wine. It leaves a damp patch on the carpet.

Standing against the wall of the very white room is the tall woman in flat shoes with the gentle American voice. She is giving the man with the white knickerbockers a recipe for bortsch. He tells her about a film he has seen recently. The woman, he says, got out of her wheelchair, took out a gun hidden in her knickers and shot the prison wardress dead. Quite an unreasonable thing to do, he says, considering she was only trying to teach the woman English. The tall woman reaches for her bag. The man takes a step backwards. She takes out a small square parcel and hands it to him. It turns out to be a water-colour painting subtitled *Coolie at the Opera*. He places this image on the wall next to Winston Churchill, and then puts his hand on her hip. The bone juts out. She traces the line of his very thin moustache. He caresses the faint blue shadows under her ice-grey eyes. It has begun to snow and the sky is swollen with the pattern of birds migrating.

As their bodies meet, perfectly, nose to nose, breast

97

to breast, pelvis to pelvis, he tells her that the night before, he broke a glass.

A LITTLE TREATISE ON
SEX AND POLITICS IN THE
1980s

I

HE WAS SITTING in the corner of Mistress Hui-Ta, a Setsuan restaurant with bamboo blinds and a waitress who wore a kilt. When Shirley opened the door she saw him. He could have been a matador run to fat, a spy, perhaps even a theatre impresario or record producer. He was in fact a wealthy businessman who owned a highly bankable avant-garde retail and design empire, two shops, a restaurant and a perfume about to be launched. He was twenty-eight years old, wore a grey silk shirt, baggy white suit and t'ai chi shoes, the soles as pristine as bleached almonds. He was sipping white wine and looked very composed. She was not to know that five minutes before (while he was waiting for her) he had spilt the wine and asked the waitress for a napkin to wipe his dripping credit cards. The waitress had changed the table-cloth with all the expediency of a mother changing a nappy.

When Shirley opened the door she saw him. He was sipping white wine and looked very composed. 'Mitzy!'

She kissed him and noted he had scented himself for her, the creases in his neck opulent and too old for his years. 'Do you think circumcised penises are less or more pleasurable than uncircumcised ones?' he asked, by means of making conversation.

Before she could reply he said very quickly, 'I don't think it makes any difference.'

'When did you last have a foreskin to know?'

He giggled, 'I do sleep with boys you know.'

They ordered pork balls and saké, observed quietly by Mistress Hui-Ta whose delicate white hands close and open in time with the tinkling wind chimes.

That same night in bed, pink sheets and black pillow-cases, he told her he didn't like the smell of sperm.

'What about all those boys you sleep with? Do they ejaculate pineapple juice?'

'That's just the sort of remark a secretary with red-gold hair and lateral leanings would make, I suppose.'

He leant over and put on the theme tune of *Dynasty* which he said helped him relax. After a while (Shirley is lying on her stomach, red-gold hair buried in the black pillow) he asked what she thought of a film called *The Fruits of Passion*.

'I'm sick of seeing women tied up and fucked.'

'Ah but where else would you get to see Klaus Kinski's scrotum?' He giggled and then, 'By the way, I love kissing you.'

meanwhile:

the glossy heads of fashion, media and business czars/czarinas occupy london taxis with a sense of having found a place for themselves in the world. it is agreed in particular social circles that being a passenger is the most desirable thing to be in the 1980s. when asked what upwardly-mobile young people like themselves vote, they say there is a difference between getting rich and getting right wing.

Mitzy took Shirley to Ibiza for a break from it all. His favourite club was called Zu. There, a man wearing a tee shirt with 'I Fuck Like A Beast' written across the front winked at her and said, 'What girl with really great brains could resist a rascal like me?' Mitzy waved at a party of young people whizzing by in a hired car and looked gleeful. 'Do you like this place Shirl?' Before she could answer he said, 'I think it's great, I mean it's appalling isn't it?' A waitress wearing nothing but a pearl G-string (left buttock tattooed) flung her arms around him. 'Mitzy Woo!' They kissed, he a little prudishly, while Shirley thought about what present to take back to her best friend Jean who also worked in the typing pool but who secretly wanted to be a ventriloquist. Jean had a doll called Rosa, and in their lunchbreaks they made up dialogue for her. Before Shirley left for Ibiza it was decided that Rosa was a broad hipped singer with uncanny instincts – but that might have changed by now.

'Am I going to model your hats for you again this year Mitzy?' the pearl-stringed waitress mumbled into the folds of his neck.

'Don't think so Pearlie. We're thinking of putting them on revolving hunks of doner kebab meat this season.'

'Those Great Greasy Donkey's Dicks?'

Shirley slunk out the door and caught a bus to a bar called Sergeant Pepper's, ordered beer and French fries and watched Max Headroom videos. Across the narrow

101

cobbled road in the fishermen's café, old men in black berets drank brandy, crutches propped against their straw chairs, exchanging stories about how they lost their limbs fighting fascism (these stories have been told many times before, in the same straw chairs), and how if they had their lives again, they would do exactly the same to fight the demon seed.

meanwhile:

health fiends wrap their political impotence in beancurd and use it as a poultice to deny their lack of direction. in fact they make beancurd a political issue.

When Shirley got back to the hotel Mitzy was talking to a group of well-designed people about his new perfume. It is to be called 'Skyscraper' and underneath, in small gold print, 'It Makes You Feel High'. They are impressed and ask him to judge Saturday's Miss Sexy Contest. He giggles, says it will be an honour, and waves goodbye as they stumble off to their third beach party before breakfast.

In the small hours she woke up to find his lips pressed into the back of her neck. In that same position he told her that his real name was Mitovska.

'By the way, I love your neck and shoulders.'

meanwhile:

people described by the government as 'economically weak' begin to get their bearings from social security offices. 'if you just tell me where the dhss building is, i'll know where i am.' before the distress of urban poverty and decay mounted its strategy of sensory deprivation, parks, churches, lamp posts, colours, smells, trees and people were also once used as maps to guide those who had lost direction.

On Saturday Mitzy judged the 'Miss Sexy Contest' and gave the winner, a six-foot weight-lifter called Brian from Bolton, a pink Swatch watch. He then agreed to an interview in the local ice-cream parlour with young media débutantes who ate cherry sorbet in between pressing buttons on their tape-recorders. 'To be upwardly mobile?' Mitzy thought for a moment and then ordered another scoop of Pecan Delight.

meanwhile:

the parents of these media débutantes doctor a tv film of orgreave to make it appear that it is the police who respond to the unprovoked violence of the pickets, rather than the contrary.

II

At the fourth Convention of Esoterics intermittent blasts of discordant notes filled the dark Camden room. Shirley talked to her old friend Carmen, a pianist who now had green hair and sat against the wall knitting a musical instrument and nibbling cumin seeds. She told Shirley she was thinking of retiring to Tuscany (Carmen is twenty-nine) where she would keep pigs as pets. Apparently, when she lived in Hungary 'all those years ago', her hosts, who owned a slaughter house, killed pigs in groups of ten every time there was a marriage in the village. Carmen felt she had a score to settle with pigs – not that she was against marriage; her own wedding took place in Nice where she and her husband went poodle chasing. In Toulouse, where they spent their honeymoon, they were so skint that Carmen prostituted herself. She said it was to buy herself and her husband reeds for their clarinets.

'Have you got the minutes of the last meeting Shirl?'
'Sure.'

The discordant melody is turned down and a French woman called Mimosa stops doing her impersonation of an anchovy. Shirley (who has volunteered to take the minutes for the last two years) passes around photocopies. The only sound in the room is the odd pistachio nut being cracked, or cigarette being lit.

TOPICS DISCUSSED REGARDING MEETING BETWEEN
POLEMIC AND AESTHETIC
AT THE FOURTH CONVENTION OF ESOTÈRICS

1 Does Oxbridge need the odd leftie with jaw line and commitment to keep the Imperial Burgundy fruity?
2 Is it OK to have orgasms if you haven't planned them?
3 Is hair mousse the new Opium of the People?
4 Is fish to chips what the hammer is to the sickle given the intervention of French fries?
5 Should aesthetic do a degree in business studies?
6 Could all polemic in the future be structured in haiku form and the dance of the syllable lead us to victory?

The secretary notes that anorexic aesthetic – felt nauseous and did in fact vomit. But she did it beautifully.

Obese polemic has promised to go on a diet and says he might even get light headed and do something silly.

Shirl. xxxx

meanwhile:

a new generation of right-wing theoreticians take on the left with an intellectual vigour unusual for conservatives, who on the whole admit they don't read, or conceal their education as a matter of etiquette – 'did the normal thing . . . nanny, harrow, cambridge'. a vision of society, the future and the past, is presented and marketed. to be a political activist begins to mean an 'agitator' or a 'troublemaker'. to be an esoteric is to be a nutter and it is therefore unlikely that anyone labelled as such will have their phones tapped. it is therefore a safe bet for the 1980s.

Christopher, the Convention of Esoterics' resident semiologist, was staring hard at Shirley's nipples and tried not to chide himself for experiencing erectile sensations from a woman's body. It made him feel like an animal. Lucinda, deep in conversation with Shirley (who had been much applauded for her diligent minute taking and awarded two bottles of genius) twirled her pale blond hair and screwed up her pale blue eyes. It was rumoured that Lucinda used to have dazzling deep blue eyes but since she got into philosophy the colour drained away. Because Christopher's eyes were fixed guiltily on Shirley's nipples he only heard fragments of their conversation, mostly Lucinda's quiet urgent voice. 'Basically I'm looking for a man and a culture whose veins are less literal. More sculptural than functional. I

require more of a place I live in than shelter, don't you?'
Shirley nodded and said she was dying for a Mars Bar.
'Do you understand what I said Shirl?'

'Sure.' Shirley nodded again and her red-gold mane
rippled down her back.

'You want to obtain an independent position outside
the structures of mass production/consumption. An
independent position often leads to a more conceptual
ideology. Chris, will you run down the road and buy
me a Mars Bar?'

'Only if you come with me.'

'Okay.'

He took her hand and they walked down the grimy
Camden Road glad of the air. He bought her a King-
Sized Mars Bar which was a bargain because it had ten
per cent extra, free.

'Do you want to come and eat your King-Sized Mars
Bar in my King-Sized Bed Shirl?'

'Okay.'

meanwhile:

bachelor writers/critics review the work of women writers;
their critical faculties academic through lack of touch and
eye contact both with human beings and their own writerly
material. as they are mostly used to doing the explaining
rather than the experiencing, this creates a problem for the
women writers who on the whole do not have this anatom-
ical split between life and art/head and heart. the women
writers decide to put a lot of sex into their writing to titillate
male editors and to mention at least one famous male poet
during the course of the narrative, although it might not be

a narrative in the religious sense of the word – perhaps
something more adulterous, like (a) plural discourse.

Shirley nibbled the last ten per cent lying in Christopher's arms. He stroked her hair marvelling at its reds
and golds, and kissed her shoulders to show that he
was not just an animal. Eyes closed, he wet his lower
lip. 'Although you and I are in bed together, there are
really four people in bed: we, the real lovers, and the
two lovers of our erotic imagination.' He licked his
finger and trailed it down her back and between her
thighs. 'When I touch you, I experience your body as
the sum of fragments.' (His finger is at last on her
nipple). 'What are you thinking Shirl?'
  'I'm thinking, life is for the lion hearted.'

meanwhile:

a man in children's sunglasses (nicknamed Hamlet) walks
the streets in torn shoes carrying a plastic bag crammed
with enormous bones ... the meat ineptly cut off so that
threads of flesh and sinew hang off the sides as if recently
scavenged. He lines them along a short broken wall at
precise distance apart.

'Life is for the lion hearted.'
  On an idle Sunday afternoon, helping Jean from the
typing pool weed her garden, Shirley realised that she
was very, very unhappy. The 'grief', as she later
described it, took hold of her quite suddenly – just as
she bent down to plant a bulb in the malnourished city
soil. She doubled up and burst into loud sobs, the bulb
naked and hard in the palm of her hand, and for some
reason the cause of her tears.

It was the thought of loving and being loved that made her sad. Later, both women lie on the grass and put on a tape of Ezra Pound reading his Cantos (XLV, LI and LXXVI). They eat oranges, stroke the cat with the torn ear, listen to Pound seek the gold in men's (and possibly women's) souls, with small lyrical incantations.

meanwhile:

a group of men sip after-hour beer in a north london pub and sing:

> what is your four o?
> i'll sing you four o
> red fly the banners high
> four for the four great masters
> three three the rights of man
> two two the man's own hands
> working for his living o
> one is worker's unity
> and ever more shall be so.

and the barmaid washing the glasses joins in with them.

III

Jean from the typing pool put a frozen pizza in the oven, poured herself a glass of sour red wine, flopped into a chair and kicked off her ostrich feather pumps. She remained in this position for about twenty minutes by which time she judged the pizza to be ready, staggered up, sighed, took out the orange and sizzling pizza, poured herself some more sour red wine, opened the cutlery drawer and took out a silver knife and fork she had inherited from her grandmother who kept a kosher kitchen. At that moment a pneumatic drill decided to penetrate the black tarmac outside the house with great shuddering screams.

Mitzy lay on Christopher and bit his lip as he orgasmed silently. Then, as if nothing had happened, he said, 'By the way, I love your buttocks and thighs.'

Jean pushed aside the remaining crusts of pizza and opened a small plastic pot of chocolate mousse. 'Rosa.' She licked the artificial cream off her fingertips, 'Rosa? Come here sweetheart.' Rosa (a wooden doll with arched eyebrows and Dietrichesque cheek-bones) reclined in the cat basket as if trying to make a difficult decision.

JEAN: What do you mean you don't want to marry him?!! Such a lovely man! Rich. Good looking. Intelligent . . .

ROSA: I don't like him grandma.

JEAN: Since when do you have to *like* the man you marry?

ROSA: I couldn't live in the same house as him.

JEAN: Then you must have *two* houses!

ROSA: But he's a fascist grandma!

JEAN: You don't have to talk politics *all* the time do you? Rosa? Answer me Rosa!! Rosa??

ROSA: I've got an orchestra of archetypal voices, grandma . . . but I've got a sore throat at the moment . . . and anyway, I can smell burning.

meanwhile:

cities in england are set on fire and looted as a protest
against white youths burning asians in their places of work
and white policemen shooting down black women in their
homes.

Mitzy threw a wild party for the staff of his fashion
empire, restaurants and perfume manufacturer. Journal-
ists, finance and admin staff, the advertising team, even
the 'boy' who came in to dust his house once a week, all
gathered in the converted warehouse where a revolving
silver ball strung from the ceiling cast small flickering
stars over their beautiful faces and bodies. Crates of
vodka were shipped over from a client in New York,
and the chef's assistant, who prided himself on his
resemblance to Scott Fitzgerald, cooked hamburgers
over live coals. He also made a large macrobiotic salad
because he liked contradictions.

'At least our prime minister's exciting ... I mean
she's so wicked ... we all can't wait to see what she'll
do next.'

A young journalist bit into his rare burger, cigarette
still smouldering in the other hand.

'Yeah. I kinda feel the same about Rambo.'

Frieda who designed most of the clothes announced
she wanted to go and take Polaroids of industrial chic,
but Mitzy (who had taken to calling his staff 'aides')
stopped her because he wanted to discuss an idea for a
dress made from ice. A second crate of vodka was
opened. Joe and Suzy, known as the 'ideal couple', came
bouncing up to Shirley, who sat alone, to tell her how
much they loved the range of imagery in her kitchen
utensils and to thank her for the dinner she had cooked

them the night before. 'We liked Jean too. I mean she's so normal she's almost weird.' Shirley sucked a strand of her red-gold hair and stared at Mitzy who was entertaining his young women shop-assistants. Through the vodka haze and hypnotic silver stars she tried to locate and understand her new 'grief'.

'Hey Shirl, are you okay?' Suzy put her arms around her.

'Do you just not feel like talking?' Joe stroked her neck. Shirley continued to stare at Mitzy on whose broad back most of the stars were swirling.

'Shirl . . . ?'

'I've got an orchestra of archetypal voices Joe and Suzy, but I've got a sore throat at the moment.'

Frieda, standing nearby drinking a Diet Pepsi, swivelled round on her seven-inch heels and took a Polaroid . . .

'Say aaaah Shirl.'

'Aaaah.'

'Your tonsils look like rubies. And again.'

'No.'

'Go on Shirl.'

'No.'

'Pleeeeeeeeeeeze.'

'AAAAAAAAAAAAAAAAAAAAAAAAAAAAAAAAAAAAAAA
AAAAAAAAAAAAAAAAAAH!!!'

meanwhile:

it is revealed there are two choices in life – to be well, or not to be well –

the president of the united states of america has a two-foot-long portion of cancerous colon removed from his intestine and a syringe full of polymorphine planted into the sheath of his spinal cord.

^Ee: A Case History

IT WAS IN retrospect presently, a terrible contradiction. It made the beating of her 25-year-old heart a day-old secret and she hoped no one else could hear, never mind see, the disquiet. If she was questioned, she predetermined her answer. It would go something like, 'I'm very well indeed thank you very very much.' But then they never asked questions – merely fed her, lightly observed what she wore each day, kept note of her mail and telephone calls.

She began to lose her gestures. It was this temporary loss of architecture that was perhaps most devastating. She could no longer paint a thought or a sentence with a brush of her hands or by widening her fish-shaped eyes. Before, this had saved her the trouble of articulating her response to their world in words. Now she had internalised her visual sense of argument there was no way to express her present state retrospectively.

She knew the birds had nowhere warm to migrate to any more. This thought made her very sad but she tried to smile for fear they thought she had a melancholy disposition.

She began to lose her hair colour. Before, this had given her some identity as a dark-haired person, but with the constant change her temperament was dictated to her and sometimes did not match her feelings.

She began to lose her family in dreams. Strange voices came out of their mouths and their limbs became fins. Her sister shrank to miniature proportions wheeling a barrow of shrivelled lemons under the Chamber of Commerce. Her mother became a rock and her father a moulting shaving-brush. This was another secret she had to keep; on the whole they thought she was recovering and she did not want to make them unhappy.

Today she is baking bread in the octagonal kitchen. The ceiling is painted entrail red and she secretly calls it the abattoir. Great care has been taken in choosing the ingredients: yogurt, almonds and coconut-milk. She knows that if an ingredient is marked with an 'E' symbol it is a danger to the continuation of the species. She also knows that they have very simple tastes and might think her extreme, so resolves to make a second loaf, this time only with salt and sesame seeds. As she kneads the dough she sets up a rhythm for herself, banging it on the wooden board. 'I'm survived ... survived ... I'm survived.' The oven is on and the warm rush of gas above her knees comforting. Today her hair is the colour of acorns and does not feel too much at odds with her mood; however, she can hear a drill being used in the next room and feels uneasy. She knows the person using it has been told to stay in and keep an eye on her. She avoids him politely; resolves after baking the bread to take some swabs of her cell tissue and then go to sleep. The drill is determined and fills her with fear. Tomorrow she is swimming in the local pool. She always keeps her eyes open under water; on dry land dust gets into her eyes and makes her itch. She tried to tell them that when they forbade her to have a bath or a shower, to tell them it was only in water she felt she had psychic immunity, but by then she had lost her gestures so she kept quiet. She finds comfort in people older than herself – like the pensioners exercising their strained bones in the shallow end. She is interested in their history. Sometimes they talk to her in the changing room and one woman made her a feather hat, cut at curious angles, especially for her.

The day before yesterday she is talking to two neighbours who chat to her about their life in Egypt. Often the wife, Lola, makes good strong coffee and they drink it upstairs smoking small Egyptian cigars, a reminder that addiction set in during those hot balmy days by the Nile. Lola wears crocodile-skin shoes and sips sweet liquers, her peroxide blond hair resisting the evolution of her seventy years. The walls of their house are covered with paintings. They are full of blood and flies, revolutionary hope and shimmering yellows. She remembers Spain is full of contradictions, recalling the graffiti on stern Malagan walls, and is talking about this when the man with the drill calls for her. He takes her away and Lola kisses her head with unusual demonstration.

The bread has risen and she is pleased. At first she did not think the yeast would rise but it has, and she even considers switching on the radio. Retrospectively in the present she decides not to; the larger wars might engulf her private war and make her lose herself again. A minor setback feeds her indecision: she has just noticed the oven is electric and not gas at all. She is taking a knife and nudging the warm bread out of the tins; she recalls a photograph of herself running across a beach, tanned and in shorts, breathless; she remembers dancing the dance of the drunken swan for her giggling brothers and sisters, ankles arched, breathless; she remembers making love to a man she loved in a caravan surrounded by Japanese geese, flushed and breathless; the loaf with the almonds is upside-down on the board.

The man with the drill comes in. He has a thin white layer of dust sprinkled on the top of his head and a dead pigeon in his pocket. She is not unaware of the strength under his tattered fisherman's smock. The loaf with the sesame seeds has got stuck in the tin and she tries to tease it out; her hands have become dull and stupid and she does not want him to be there. He tells her she has been spending too much time in the bath and spikes a steel syringe into the warm belly of the struggling loaf of bread.

Already she is reading her fortune in cups of seaweed and plankton. She is thinking about a riddle her mother set her: 'What's a quarter of a century between sisters?' A mere synopsis.

The sesame bread has come apart and lies in two pieces next to the almond bread. The man with the drill has led her to her room and kindly fluffed the white pillows for her. He promises her a slice of the bread she made, but only at the right time.